"You're embarrassed by how strong the attrac... ...uced after wa... He sounded...

Gwyn's ston... ...usness. ...ould her fa...

...his releasing of compromising photos is very ...shrewd," he said in an abrupt shift. His tone ...uggested it was an item in political news, not a ...gross defilement of her personal self. His finger rested across his lips in contemplation.

"Jensen has very cleverly made himself appear a victim," he said. "Whatever story he comes up with, it will point all the scandal back to you and the bank."

"I'm aware that my life is over, thanks," she bit out.

"Nothing is over," he said with a cold-blooded smile. "Jensen landed a punch, but I will hit back. Hard. You must want to set things straight? If so, you'll help me make it clear you had zero romantic interest in Jensen."

"How?" she choked, wondering what was in his drink that he thought he could accomplish that.

"By going public with our *own* affair."

Canadian **Dani Collins** knew in high school that she wanted to write romance for a living. Twenty-five years later, after marrying her high school sweetheart, having two kids with him, working at several generic office jobs and submitting countless manuscripts, she got "The Call." Her first Modern Romance novel won the Reviewers' Choice Award for Best First in Series from *RT Book Reviews.* She now works in her own office, writing romance.

Books by Dani Collins

Harlequin Presents

Vows of Revenge
Seduced into the Greek's World
The Russian's Acquisition
An Heir to Bind Them
A Debt Paid in Passion
More than a Convenient Marriage?
No Longer Forbidden?

The Wrong Heirs

The Marriage He Must Keep
The Consequence He Must Claim

Seven Sexy Sins

The Sheikh's Sinful Seduction

The 21st Century Gentleman's Club

The Ultimate Seduction

One Night With Consequences

Proof of their Sin

Visit the Author Profile page at Harlequin.com for more titles.

Dani Collins

BOUGHT BY HER ITALIAN BOSS

Recycling programs for this product may not exist in your area.

ISBN-13: 978-0-373-13451-9

Bought by Her Italian Boss

First North American Publication 2016

This edition published by arrangement with Harlequin Books S.A.

For questions and comments about the quality of this book, please contact us at CustomerService@Harlequin.com.

Printed in U.S.A.

BOUGHT BY HER ITALIAN BOSS

For my editor, Kathryn,
because she "loved, loved, loved" it.

CHAPTER ONE

GWYN ELLIS LOOKED from the screen to Nadine Billaud, the public relations manager for Donatelli International, then back to the screen.

"This is you, *oui*?" Nadine prodded.

Gwyn couldn't speak. Her heart had begun slamming inside her rib cage the moment she had recognized herself. Cold sweat coated her skin. Air wouldn't squeeze past her locked throat, let alone words.

That *was* her. *Naked.* Right there on that computer, the line of her bare bottom clear as the crack of dawn, neatly framed by her hot pink thong. Everyone had a backside that looked more or less like that, but she was extremely selective about showing hers to *anyone*. She certainly didn't email shots like this to men she barely knew. Or post them online.

Her whole body felt like a frozen electrical current was vibrating through her, paralyzing her.

The photo changed and that bare torso with the sheet rumpled across her upper thighs was all her, too. The way her breasts lifted as she arched her back and ran fingers through her hair bordered on deliberately erotic, coupled with that blissful, upturned expression. She looked like she'd been making love all day—as if she even knew what that felt like!

Then the final one came up again. She was adjusting the band of her hot pink undies across her cocked hip, looking like she was teasingly deciding whether to keep them on or remove them, eyes still lazily drooped and soft satisfaction painted across her lips.

The lighting was golden and her skin faintly gleamed—with oil, she realized as her brain began to function past the shock. These had been taken at the spa where she'd had a massage, trying to fix the ache between her shoulder blades that had been torturing her for weeks. She was sitting up and dressing after her appointment, relaxed and comfortable in what she had perceived as complete privacy.

The massage table had been cropped from the images, leaving muted sage-green walls and indistinct, blurred flowers in the background. It could have been a hotel room, a bedroom—whatever the viewer wanted to imagine.

Her stomach roiled. She thought she might be hyperventilating because she could hear a distant hiss. She wanted to throw up, pass out, *die. Please God, take me now.*

"Mademoiselle?" Nadine badgered.

"Yes," she stammered. "It's me." Then, as the sheer

mortification of the whole thing struck, she added a strident, *"Can you close that, please?"*

She glanced at Signor Fabrizio, her supervisor. He sat next to her with a supercilious expression on his middle-aged face.

"Why are you showing those like that? With him in here?" Gwyn asked. "Couldn't we have done this privately?"

"They're available to anyone with an online connection. I've seen them," Fabrizio said pithily. "I brought them to Nadine's attention."

He'd already taken a long look? *Gross.*

Tears hit her eyes like the cut of a hard, biting wind. An equally brutal blow seemed to land in her stomach, pushing nausea higher into the back of her throat.

"Surely you knew this could happen when you took those photos and sent them to Mr. Jensen?" Nadine said.

Nadine had kept her snooty nose high in the air from the moment Gwyn had followed Fabrizio into her office. Fabrizio kept giving her darkly smug looks, like he was staring right through her perfectly respectable blue pencil skirt and matching jacket.

He made her skin crawl.

And worry for her job. Her palms were sweating.

"I didn't take those photos," she said as strongly as her tight throat would allow. "And you think I would send something like that to a client? They're—oh, for the love of God." She heard the door opening behind her and shot to her feet, reaching to push the lid of Nadine's laptop down herself, wishing the images could be quashed that easily.

Deep in the back of her psyche, she knew she was going to cry. Soon. Pressure was building behind her collarbone, compressing her lungs, pushing behind her eyes. But for the moment she was in a type of shock. Like she'd been shot and still had the strength to run before the true depth of her injuries debilitated her.

"Signor Donatelli." Nadine rose. "Thank you for coming."

"You notified him?" Signor Fabrizio jerked to his feet, sounding dismayed.

Whatever remained of Gwyn's composure went into free fall. The *owner* of the bank was here? She tried to gather herself to face yet another denigrating expression.

"It's protocol with something this dangerous to the bank's reputation," Nadine said stiffly, adding to the weight on Gwyn's heart.

"She's being dismissed," Fabrizio hurried to assure Signor Donatelli. "I was about to tell her to collect her things."

Time stopped as Gwyn processed that she was being fired. Stupid her, she had thought she was being called in to talk about a client's possible misappropriation of funds, not to be disgraced in front of the entire world.

Literally the entire world. This was what online

bullying felt like. This was persecution. A witch hunt. Stoning. She couldn't take in how monumentally unjust this was.

The only experience she could liken it to was when her mother had been diagnosed. Words were being said, facts stated that couldn't be denied, but she had no real grasp of how the next minute or week or the rest of her life would play out from this moment forward.

She didn't want to face it, but she had no choice.

And the silence around her told her they were all waiting for her to do so.

Very slowly, she turned to the man who'd just entered, but it wasn't Paolo Donatelli, president and head of the family that owned Donatelli International. No, it was far worse.

Vittorio Donatelli. Paolo's cousin, second-in-command as VP of operations. A man of, arguably, even more stunningly good looks, at least in her estimation. His features were as refined and handsome as his Italian heritage demanded. He was clean-shaven, excruciatingly well dressed in a tailored suit and wore an air of arrogance that came as much from his lean height as his aloof expression. His ability to dominate any situation was obvious in the way they all stood in silence, waiting for him to speak.

He didn't know her from Adam, she knew that. She'd smiled brightly at him not long after arriving here in Milan, forgetting that secret crushes didn't know they were the object of such yearnings. He'd looked right through her and it had stung. Quite badly, illogically.

"Nadine. Oscar," Vittorio said with a brief flick of his gaze to the other occupants of the room before coming back to give Gwyn a piercing stare from his bronze eyes.

Her heart gave a skip between pounds, reacting to him even when she was verging on hysteria. Her mouth was so dry she couldn't make it stretch into a smile. She doubted she would ever smile again. The strange buzz inside her intensified.

"Miss Ellis," he said with a hostile nod of acknowledgment.

He knew her name from Nadine's report, she supposed. The furious accusation in his eyes told her he'd seen the photos. Of course he'd seen them. That's why he had stooped from the lofty heights of the top floor to the midlevel of the Donatelli Tower.

Gwyn's shallow breaths halted and her knees quivered. She was weirdly shocked by how defenseless the idea of his seeing her naked made her feel, but the effect this very perfect stranger had had on her from the start was unprecedented. She'd seen him stride through the offices in Charleston once and that simple glimpse of an incredibly handsome and dynamic man had made her view the postings at the head office in Milan that much more favorably than any other branch in the organization. She had wanted to advance, would have taken whatever promotions she could land, but this was her dream location.

Because it gave her the chance to see him.

Be careful what you wish for. She mashed her lips together into a hard, steady line, heart scored, then turned her face away, trying to recover.

He was, quite obviously, nothing like the man she'd constructed in her mind. Italian men were warm and gregarious and adored women, she had thought, expecting he'd flirt with her if they ever actually spoke. She had expected him to give her a chance to intrigue him, despite the fact that she worked for him.

But the man she had been obsessing over had not only glimpsed her naked, he was completely unmoved by what he'd seen. He was repelled. Blamed her. Was privately calling her a whore and worse—

She stopped herself from spiraling. The pieces of her shattered world were being kicked around enough. She had to keep a grip.

But she wasn't used to being rejected out of hand, seeing no interest whatsoever from a man. The reaction was usually the opposite. Her body had always pulled a certain amount of male attention. She didn't encourage it and was pretty boring personality-wise. She worked in *banking*, for heaven's sake. Her hair was the most common brown you could find and she wasn't terribly pretty. Her face was only elevated from plain to pleasant by her mother's exceptionally good skin and a cheery nature that usually kept a smile on her mouth. So she shouldn't be that surprised when a man who could have his pick of women showed no interest in her.

It made her ache all the same.

Think, she ordered herself, but it was hard when she was stuck in this swamp of feeling so thoroughly scorned by a man who enthralled her.

"I want a lawyer," she managed to say.

"Why would you need one?" Vittorio asked with a wrathful lift of his brows, so godlike.

"This is wrongful dismissal. You're treating me like a criminal when those photos are illegal. They were taken at a spa without my knowledge. They're not selfies, so how could I have sent them to Kevin Jensen? Or anyone? His wife is the one who recommended I go there for my shoulder!"

Vito flicked his gaze to the laptop, mentally reviewing images that would have been very titillating if they were a private communication between lovers. For long seconds as he'd reviewed the photos, he'd been captivated against his will, having to force himself to move past his transfixion with her sensual figure to the fact that this was a hydrogen bomb aimed directly at the bank that was his livelihood and the foundation that supported his entire extended family.

But the photos weren't selfies. That was true. He had thought Jensen must have taken them.

Nadine seemed to think his shift of attention was a prompt for her to bring them up for another look. She started to open her laptop.

"Would you stop showing those to people, you freak?" Gwyn cried.

"Let's keep this professional," Nadine snapped.

"How would you react if you were me?" Gwyn shot back.

Gwyn Ellis was not what he had expected. There was an American wholesomeness to her that neutralized some of the femme fatale that had come across on-screen. He had expected, and received, an impact of female sexuality when he had entered the room. He'd felt the same thing the day she'd smiled at him in the lobby.

She'd already been under suspicion, so he'd pretended not to notice her, but nothing could downplay her allure. That body of hers didn't stop, with her firm, well-rounded breasts that sat high beneath her neatly cut jacket and her waistline that begged for a man's hands to clasp before sliding down to the flare of her hips and her gorgeously plump ass that he dreamed of kneading. Knees were not something he'd normally catalogue, but she had cute ones.

An image of cupping them as he held them apart drifted through his brain.

She was a very potent woman. Her shoulders were stiff, her frame tense and defensive, but her slight stature and smooth curves announced to the animal kingdom that she was undeniably a female of the species, of fertile age and irresistibly ripe.

She called to the male in him, quickening the blood of the beast that he suppressed at all costs.

Visceral reactions like lust were something he indulged in very controlled quantities. This was not the time and, judging by his reaction to her, Gwyn was not the woman. High-octane risk-taking was his cousin's bailiwick. Vito controlled his bloodlust ruthlessly—even though there was a part of him that beat with excitement for the challenge of throwing himself into this perfect storm of chemistry to see if he could survive it.

What they could do to one another…

He turned his mind from speculating, hearing Nadine aim a very pointed barb at Gwyn. "I wouldn't sleep with a married man. This wouldn't happen to me."

"Who said I slept with Kevin Jensen?" Gwyn challenged hotly. "*Who?* I want a name."

So indignant. This was not the reaction of a woman who had posed for a lover, running the risk of exposure. She ought to be furious with Jensen or his wife, perhaps tossing her hair in defiance of judgment over her decision to pose naked for her paramour. Instead, she was a woman on the edge of her control, reacting to a catastrophe with barely contained hysteria.

"His wife said you slept with him. Or want to. Obviously," Oscar Fabrizio interjected, "since she posted these filthy photos when she discovered them on his phone. You've been having lunches and dinners with him."

Vito found that attack interesting. He had brought

certain suspicions about their nonprofit accounts manager to Paolo's attention a few weeks ago. The assumption had easily been made that the New Girl was in on the arrangement, facilitating.

"Kevin wanted to do things—have our meetings, I mean," Gwyn quickly clarified, "away from the office." She was visibly distraught, looking to Vito in entreaty. "He's a client. I didn't have a choice but to go to him if that's what he requested."

Vito had to accept that. Excellence of customer service was a cornerstone at Donatelli International. If a client of Jensen's caliber wanted a house call, employees were expected to make them.

"You didn't take those photos?" he pressed her.

"No!"

"So they're not on that phone?" He nodded at where she clutched her device in a death grip.

Gwyn had forgotten she was holding it, but she always grabbed it out of habit when she left her desk, and had switched it to silent as she came into this meeting. Now she stared at it, surprised to see it there. At least she could say with confidence, "No. They're not."

"You'll let me confirm that?" He held out his hand.

On the surface it was a very reasonable request, but, oh, dear Lord, *no*. She had something on here that was beyond embarrassing. It would make this situation so much worse… *So much worse.*

She knew her face was falling into lines of panicked guilt, but couldn't help it.

His nostrils flared and his jaw hardened. The death rays coming out of his eyes told her she'd be lucky to merely lose her job.

"This phone is mine," she stammered, trying not to let him intimidate her. If she hadn't already been violated, she might not have been so vehement, but he was going to have to knock her out cold to pry this thing out of her hand if he wanted access. "I get an allowance to offset my using it for company business, but it's mine. You don't have any right to look at it."

"Can it clear you of suspicion or not?" His gaze delved into her culpable one.

She couldn't hide the turmoil and resentment coursing through her at being put on the spot. "My privacy has been invaded enough."

She was naked. On the internet. She supposed everyone in the building was staring at her image right now. Men saying filthy, suggestive things. Women judging whether her stomach was flat enough, saying she had cellulite, calling her too bony or too tall or too something so they could feel better about their own body issues.

Gwyn wanted to hang her head and sob.

All she could think was how hard she'd worked not to be pushed around by life the way her mother had been. At every stage, she'd tried to be self-reliant, autonomous, control her future.

Breathe, she commanded herself. *Don't think about it.* She would fall apart. She really would.

"I think we have our answer," Fabrizio said pitilessly.

She was starting to hate that man. Gwyn wasn't the type to hate. She did her best to get along with everyone. She was a happy person, always believing that life was too short for drama and conflict. Being the first to apologize made her the bigger person, she had always thought, but she doubted she would ever forgive these people for how they were treating her right now.

A muted buzz sounded and Nadine looked at her own phone. "The press is gathering. We need to make a statement."

The press? Gwyn circled around Fabrizio to the window and looked down.

Nadine's office was midway up the tower, but the crowd at the entrance, and the cameras they held, were like ants pouring out of a disturbed hill. It was as bad as a royal birth down there.

She swallowed, stomach turning again.

Kevin Jensen was an icon, a modern day, international superhero who flew into disaster aftermath to offer "feet on the ground" assistance. Anyone with half a brain saw that he exploited heart-wrenching situations on camera to increase donations and boost his own profile, but the bottom line was he showed up to terrible tragedies and brought aid. He did real, necessary work for the devastated.

But lately Gwyn had been questioning how he spent some of those abundant donations.

Had this been his answer? A massive discrediting that would get her fired?

She hugged herself. This sort of thing didn't happen to real people. Did it?

Her gaze searched below for an escape route. She couldn't even leave the building to get to her rented flat here in Milan. How would she get back to America? Even if she got that far, then what? Look to her stepfather to shelter her? Who was going to hire her with this sort of notoriety? Ever?

She'd be exactly what she'd tried so hard to avoid being: a burden. A leach.

Oh, God...oh, God. The walls were beginning to creak and buckle around her composure. The pressure behind her cheekbones built along with weight on her shoulders and upper arms.

Nadine was talking as she typed, "…say that the bank was unaware of this personal relationship and the employee has been terminated—"

"Our client has stated that the photos were *not* invited," Fabrizio interjected.

Gwyn spun around. "And your employee states that she's been targeted by a peeping tom and an online porn peddler and a vengeful wife."

Nadine paused only long enough to send her a stern look. "I strongly advise you not to speak to the press."

"I strongly advise you that I will be speaking to a lawyer." It was an empty threat. Her savings were very modest. *Very.* Much as she would love to believe her stepbrother would help her, she couldn't count on it. He had his own corporate image to maintain.

The way Vittorio Donatelli continued to emanate hostility made her want to crawl into a hole and die.

"How long have you been with the company?" Nadine asked.

"Two years in Charleston, four months here," Gwyn said, trying to recall how much room her credit card balance had for plane fare and setting up house back in Charleston. Not enough.

"Two years," Nadine snorted, adding an askance. "How did you earn a promotion like this after only that short a time?" Her gaze skimmed down Gwyn's figure, clearly implying that Gwyn had slept her way into the position. Night school and language classes and putting in overtime counted for nothing, apparently.

Fabrizio didn't defend her, despite signing off on her transfer and giving her a glowing review after her first three months.

Vittorio's expression was an inscrutable mask. Was he thinking the same thing?

A disbelieving sob escaped her and she hugged herself, trying to stay this side of manic.

While Vittorio brought his own phone from his pants pocket and with a sweep and tap connected to someone. "Bruno? Vito. I need you in Nadine Billaud's office. Bring some of your men."

"For my walk of shame?" Gwyn presumed. Here came the tears, welling up like a tsunami with a mile of volume behind it. Her voice cracked. "Don't worry. I plan to leave quickly and quietly. I can't *wait* to not work here anymore."

"You'll stay right here until I tell you to leave." His tone was implacable, making her heart sink in her hollow chest while another part of her rose in defiance, wanting to fight and rail and physically tear at him to get out of here. She was the quintessential wounded animal that needed to bolt from danger to its cave.

To Nadine, he added, "Confirm the photos belong to one of our employees. For privacy and legal reasons we have no other comment. Ask the reporters to disperse and enlist the lobby guards to help. Issue a similar statement to all employees. Add a warning that they risk termination if they speak to the press or are observed viewing the photos on corporate equipment or company grounds. Oscar, I need a full report on how these photos came to your attention."

"Signor Jensen contacted me this morning—"

"Not here." Vittorio moved to the door as a knock sounded. "In your office. Wait here," he said over his shoulder to Gwyn, like she was a dog to be left at home while he went to work. He urged the other two from the room and pulled the door closed behind the three of them.

"Yeah, right," Gwyn rasped into the silence of Nadine's empty office, hugging herself so tightly she was suffocating.

A twisting, writhing pain moved in her like a

snake, coiling around her organs to squeeze her heart and lungs, tightening her stomach and closing her throat. She covered her face, trying to hide from the terrible reality that everyone—everyone in the world—was not only staring at her naked body, but believing that she had had sex with a married man.

She could live with people staring at her body. Almost. They did it, anyway. But she was a good person. She didn't lie or steal or come on to men, especially married ones! She was conservative in the way she lived her life, saving her craziest impulses for things like her career where she did wildly ambitious things like sign up for Mastering Spreadsheets tutorials in hopes of moving up the ladder.

The pressure in her cheekbones and nose and under her eyes became unbearable. She tried to press it back with the flats of her hands, but a moan of anguish was building from the middle of her chest. A sob bounced like a hard pinball, bashing against her inner walls, moving up from her breastbone into her throat.

She couldn't break down, she reminded herself. Not here. Not yet. She had to get out of this place and the sooner the better. It was going to be awful. A nightmare, but she would do it, head high and under her own steam.

Gritting her teeth, she reached for the door and started to open it.

A burly man wearing a suit and a short, neat haircut was standing with his back to the door. Guarding her? He grabbed the doorknob, keeping her from pulling it open. His body angled enough she could see he also wore some kind of clear plastic earpiece. His glance at her was both indifferent and implacable.

"Attendere qui, per favore." Wait here, please.

She was so shocked, she let him pull the door from her lax grip and close her into Nadine's office again.

Actually, it slipped freely from her clammy hand. The room began to feel very claustrophobic. She moved to the window again, seeing the crowd of reporters had grown. She couldn't tell if Nadine was addressing them. She could hardly see. Her vision was blurring. She sniffed, feeling the weight of all that had happened so deeply she had to move to the nearest chair and sink into it.

Her breath hitched and no amount of pressure from her hands would push back the burn behind her eyes.

The door opened again, startling her heart into lurching and her head into jerking up.

He was back.

CHAPTER TWO

GWYN ELLIS LOOKED like hell had moved in where her soul used to be, eyes pits of despair, mouth soft and bracketed by lines of disillusion. Her brow was a crooked line of suffering, but she immediately sat taller, blinking and visibly fighting back her tears to face him without cowering.

"I want to leave," she asserted.

The rasp in her voice scraped at his nerves while he studied her. Vixens knew how to use their sexuality on a man. If she was a victim, he would expect her to appeal to the protector in him. Either way, he wouldn't expect her to be so confrontational.

Gwyn was a fighter. He didn't want to find that dig-deep-and-stay-strong streak in her admirable. It softened him when he was in crisis control mode, trying to remember that she had, quite possibly, colluded to bilk the bank and a completely legitimate nonprofit organization of millions of euros in donations.

"We have more to talk about," he told her. He had

made the executive decision to question her himself, like this, privately. And he wasn't prepared to ask himself why.

"An exit interview? I have two short words," she said tightly.

That open hostility was noteworthy. Oscar Fabrizio had been full of placating statements until Paolo had been patched through on speakerphone. Then Oscar had seemed to realize he was under suspicion. He'd asked for a lawyer. Sweat had broken across his brow and upper lip when Vito had ordered his computer and phone to be analyzed. Both were company issued and it had been obvious Oscar was dying to contact someone—Kevin Jensen perhaps? A plainclothes investigator was on the way. A full criminal inquiry was being launched down the hall.

While here…Vito was sure she was an accomplice, except…

"You say you had no knowledge of those photos," he challenged.

"No. I didn't." Her chin came up and her lashes screened her eyes, but there was no hiding the quiver of her mouth. She was deeply upset about their being made public. That was not up for dispute. "They were taken after a massage. I didn't know there was a camera in the room."

The images were imprinted on his brain. The photos would have made a splash without Jensen's name attached, he thought distantly. She was built like Venus.

But he saw how they could have been taken during a private moment and manipulated to appear like shots between lovers. He had made certain presumptions on sight: that she was not only having an affair with a client, but was engaged in criminal activity with him. If Jensen was prepared to steal from charity donations, would it be such a stretch to photograph a banking underling in an attempt to cover it up?

Powerful men exploited young, vulnerable women. He knew that. It was quite literally in his DNA.

"Are you picturing me naked?" she challenged bitterly, but her chin crinkled and she fought for her composure a moment, then bravely firmed her mouth and controlled her expression, meeting his gaze with loathing shadowing the depths of her brown eyes.

Such a contrary woman with her wounded expression and quiet, forest-creature coloring of dark eyes and hair, then that devastatingly powerful figure of generous curves and lissome limbs.

"Wondering if you are having an affair with Jensen," he replied.

"I'm not!" There was a catch in her voice before her tone strengthened. "And I wasn't trying to start one, either. I barely know him." She crossed her arms. "I actually think he's been skimming funds from his foundation for himself."

"He is." He steadily returned the shocked brown stare she flashed at him. Her irises had a near-black rim around the dark chocolate brown, he noted, liking the directness it added to her subtly tough demeanor.

Her pupils expanded with surprise, further intriguing him.

"You know that for a fact?" Her brows were like distant bird wings against the sky, long and elegant with a perfect little crook above her eyes. She was truly beautiful.

He wanted her. Badly.

He ignored the need pulling at him, stating, "We also know someone in the bank is colluding with him. We've been conducting an extremely delicate investigation that blew up today, thanks to your photos."

Vito was angry with himself. He was a numbers man, calculating all the odds, all the possible moves an opponent might try, but he hadn't seen this one coming.

"I'm not colluding with anyone!" Her expression was earnest and very convincing. But he was a mistrustful man at heart, too aware of the secrets and lies he lived under himself to take for granted that other people weren't self-protecting or withholding certain facts to better their own position.

"And yet you won't let me look at your phone," he said pointedly.

Her jaw set and she turned the device over in her hands. With a shaky little sigh that smacked of defeat, she tapped in her access code, surprising him with her sudden willingness.

"Look at my emails," she urged. "You'll see I was

counseling him that certain requests could b
preted as shady." She offered him the phone.

Gwyn didn't know much about climbing out of a hole, but she knew you had to bounce off rock bottom, so she went there. At least this humiliation was her choice and only between the two of them, now that the room was empty. At least she was getting a chance to speak her side. Maybe he'd see that she didn't have anything to hide except a stupid attraction. Hopefully he'd read between the lines and also see that she wasn't the least bit interested in stupid Kevin Jensen.

Still, it was hard to sit here with the anticipation of further shame washing over her. He would see that her handful of texts and emails with friends back home were innocuous and seldom. She was friendly with many, but actual friends with very few. It was a symptom of moving so much through her childhood, as her mother had tried to find better positions for herself. Gwyn kept in touch with people she liked, mostly through social media, but she didn't bond very often. She had learned early that it hurt too much when she had to move on. The person she was closest to, her stepfather, didn't "do" computers. They talked the old-fashioned way, over the phone or face-to-face.

If Vittorio glanced through her social media accounts, he'd see she followed liberal pundits and quirky celebrities. If he looked at her apps, he'd discover she kept her checking account in the black, played Sudoku when she was bored, read mostly romance and had finished her period three days ago.

And if he looked at her photos, he'd see that she had been taking in the sights of Milan on lunches and weekends. Sights that included his extremely handsome head shot hanging in the main foyer of the Donatelli International building.

Her cheeks stung as she waited out his discovery of the incriminating photo. She'd taken it in a fit of infatuation the other day. After passing the fountain in the lobby a million times since her arrival, she'd noticed someone taking a selfie with the burbling water in the background. It had made her realize she could *pretend* to take a selfie and capture the image of her obsession on the wall.

Why? Why had she followed through on such a silly impulse? It had been as mature as pinning up a poster of a movie star in her bedroom and talking to it.

Especially when he'd been so dismissive the one time she'd smiled at him, like he couldn't imagine why she, a lowly minion, would send such a dazzling welcome his direction. He worked at such a high level in the bank, he barely showed up to the offices at all. He didn't consort with peasants like her.

How many times had she even seen him since arriving here? Four?

She mentally snorted at herself. Like she hadn't counted each glimpse as if they were days until Christmas. She looked for him all the time. It was a bit of a sickness, really. Why? What on earth had convinced her that she had anything in common with a man like him?

Her heightened awareness of him picked up on the subtle stillness that overcame him.

She refused to look at him, certain he was staring at his own image. He must be thinking she was a weird, stalker type now. By any small miracle, was he also noticing that she didn't have those stupid nudes on there?

"Today is full of surprises." Vittorio clicked off her phone and tucked it into his shirt pocket, drawing her startled glance. His hammered-gold eyes held an extra glitter of male speculation, something dark and predatory, like he'd just noticed the plump bird that had landed nearby.

Her stomach swooped.

"Did you read the emails?" she asked shakily.

"I glanced over them."

"And?"

"They appear to support your claim that you weren't involved."

"*Appear* to support," she repeated. "Like I wrote those emails as some kind of premeditated attempt to cover my butt?" Her translucent skin was growing pink with temper. "Look, you have to know it's tricky to tell a client an outright 'no.' I've been trying to do it nicely while Mr. Jensen and Signor Fabrizio—"

Her face blanked. She touched between her furrowed brow.

"They've been setting me up this whole time, haven't they? That's why I got this promotion. They thought I was too inexperienced to see what they were up to. As soon as I proved I wasn't, they turned me into their fall guy. They just pushed me off the roof!"

She was very convincing, right down to the way her trembling hand moved to cover her mouth and her eyes glassed with anxious outrage.

He tried to hang on to his cynicism, but he was entertaining similar thoughts. The very idea ignited a strange fury in him. He knew better than most what happened when a corrupt man took advantage of an ingenuous woman. His father had done it to his mother and she had wound up dead.

His phone vibrated. He glanced at the text from his cousin. Fabrizio claims it was all her. Any progress on your end?

Vito glanced at Gwyn, at the way her shaking fingers smoothed her hair behind her ear while her concubine mouth pouted with very credible fear.

He wasn't without concern himself. Even if Paolo managed to build a case against Fabrizio, Kevin Jensen had positioned himself very well to walk away along the high ground, leaving the bank wearing a cloak of muddied employees. An institution that staked its success on a reputation of trustworthiness would cease to appear so.

Vito refused to let that happen. He protected his

family at all costs. They would, and had, done the same for him.

And this *would* cost him. Gwyn was dangerous. The fact that he was drawn to her, looking to see her as an innocent despite the very real fact she might be involved in crimes against the bank, was unnerving. Being close to her would be a serious test of his mettle.

But his glimpse into her phone had revealed a move to him that even a master chess player like Kevin Jensen wouldn't see coming, even though it was one of the basic rules of the game: if a pawn was pushed far enough into the field of play, she could be promoted to a formidable queen.

CHAPTER THREE

VITTORIO PLUCKED HIS handkerchief from his jacket pocket and moved to dampen it under the tap of the water cooler.

Gwyn watched him, wondering what he was doing, then noticed her purse was over his shoulder, looking incongruous against his tailored charcoal suit.

"Did you get my stuff from my desk?"

Fabrizio seeing her naked was creepy. Vittorio touching her possessions was…*intimate*. Disturbing.

"I did." He came back to tilt up her chin and started to run a blessedly cool, damp, linen-wrapped fingertip beneath her eye.

His touch sent an array of sensation outward through her jawline and down her throat, warm tingles that unnerved her. She tried to jerk away, but he firmed his hold and finished tidying her makeup, telling her, "Hold your head high as we walk to the elevator."

His tone was commanding, his mouth a stern line,

while he gave her a circumspect look and tucked a loose strand of her hair behind her ear.

She knocked his hand away, chest tightening again. "I just explained that they're using me. You won't even take a second to consider that might be true? You're just going to fire me and throw me to the wolves?"

"Your termination can't be helped, Gwyn. I have to think about the bank."

His detached tone sent a spike of ice right into her heart. "Thanks a lot."

They wound up in another stare down that pulled her already taut nerves to breaking point. She hated that he was standing while she was still seated. He seemed to have all the power, all the control and advantage.

She hated that, with their gazes locked like this, her mind turned to sexual awareness, refusing to let her stay in a state of fixed hatred. She wondered things like how his lips would feel against hers and grew hot as an allover body flush simmered against the underside of her skin.

She stood abruptly, forcing him to take a step back.

"Good girl," he said, moving to the door.

"I'm not *obeying* you. I—" She cut herself off. She wanted to leave, she did. She wanted to lock herself in her flat where she could lick her wounds and figure out what to do next.

"The reporters won't leave until you do," he said heartlessly. "People will be trying to go for lunch."

Don't inconvenience the staff with your petty disaster of a life, Gwyn. Think of others in the midst of your crisis.

"Everyone's going to stare," she mumbled, trying to find her guts, but her insides were nothing but water.

"They will," he agreed, still completely unmoved. "But it's only two minutes of your life. Look straight ahead. Come. Now."

Her heels wanted to root to the floor in protest. She wanted to beg him to let her hide here until after closing, but he was right. Better to get it over with.

She knew then what it was like to walk toward execution. While her low heels took her closer to the door, her heart began slamming in panic. Sweat cooled the ardor she'd experienced a moment ago, leaving her in something close to shock.

She sought refuge in her old yoga lessons, concentrating on breathing in through her nose, out through her narrowly parted lips, holding reality at bay, picturing the crown of her head being pulled by an invisible wire toward the ceiling.

"Good," Vittorio said as he opened the door, then settled his arm around her, tucking her shoulder under his armpit as his hand took possession of her waist.

She stiffened in surprise at the contact. A disconcerting rush of heat blanketed her, making her knees weaken.

He supported her, forcing her forward and keeping her on her feet when she would have stumbled. He matched their steps perfectly, as though they had walked as a couple many times before.

Two minutes, she repeated to herself, leaning into him despite how much she resented him. She'd never realized how long a minute was until she had to bear the rustle of heads turning and chairs squeaking, conversation stopping and keyboard tapping halting into a blanket of silence.

Vittorio's aftershave, spicy and beguiling, enveloped her. It was dizzying. An assault to already overloaded senses. Were her legs going to hold her? Amazing how being escorted like this made you feel like a criminal as well as look like one.

Her eyes were seared blind. She couldn't tell who was looking, couldn't really see the rest of the open-plan office because Vittorio kept her on his side closest to the wall and stayed a quarter step ahead of her so his big shoulders blocked her vision of the rest of the floor.

Another man paced on his far side, broad and burly and carrying a file box that held a green travel cup that she thought might be hers. Had they also collected the snapshot of her with her mother and stepfather, she worried?

The elevator was being held open by another hit-man type with a buzz cut. He couldn't care less about her silly scandal, his watchful indifference seemed to say. He was here to bust heads if anyone stepped out of line.

The elevator closed and she let out her breath, but rather than dropping as she expected, the elevator climbed, making her stagger and clutch instinctively at Vittorio's smooth jacket.

He cradled her closer, steadying her, fingers moving soothingly at her waist. Disturbing her with the intimacy of his touch.

"Why aren't we going down?" she asked shakily.

"The helicopter will avoid the scrum."

"Helicopter?" she choked out, mind scattering as she tried to make sense of this turn of events.

"Thirty seconds," he warned, tone gruff, and nudged her a step forward as the elevator leveled out with a *ding*.

His arm remained firm across her back, urging her through the opening doors.

She trembled, trying not to fold into him, but he was the only solid thing in her world right now. She had to remember that despite his seeming solicitude, he wasn't on her side. This was damage control. Nothing more.

The refinement at this height in the building was practically polished into the stillness of the air. Nevertheless, humans were humans. Heads came up. Eyes followed.

Vittorio addressed no one, only steered her down a hall in confident, unhurried steps, past a boardroom of men in suits and women with perfectly coiffed hair, past a lounge where a handful of people stood drinking coffee and into a glass receiving area beyond which a helicopter stood, rotors beginning to turn.

The security guard took her box of possessions ahead of them and tucked it into a bulkhead, then moved into the cockpit.

Wow. This wasn't a helicopter like she'd seen on television, where people were crammed into three seats across the back wall, shoulder to shoulder, and had to put on headphones and shout to be heard.

This was an executive lounge that belonged on a yacht. She didn't have to duck as she moved into it. The white leather seats were ten times plusher than the very expensive recliner she'd purchased for her stepfather two Christmases ago. The seats rotated, she realized, as Vittorio pointed her to one, then turned another so they would sit facing each other.

There was a door to the pilot's cockpit, like on an airplane. An air hostess smiled a greeting and nodded at Vittorio, taking a silent order from him that he gave with the simple raising of two fingers. She arrived seconds later with two drinks that looked suspiciously like scotch, neat.

Vittorio lowered a small table between them with indents to hold their glasses.

Gwyn took a deep drink of her scotch, shivering as the burn chased down her throat, then replaced her glass into its holder with a dull thud. "Where are you taking me?"

"This isn't a kidnapping," he said dryly. "We're

going to Paolo's home on Lake Como. It's in his wife's name and not on the paparazzi's radar."

"What? No," she insisted, reaching to open her seatbelt. "My passport is in my apartment. I need it to get home."

"To America? The press there is more relentless than ours. Even if you managed to drop out of sight, I would still have an ugly smudge on the bank's reputation to erase."

"I care as much about the bank as it does about me," she informed him coldly.

"Please stay seated, Gwyn. We're lifting off." He pointed to where the horizon lowered beneath them. "Let's talk about your photo of *me*."

A fresh blush rose hotly from the middle of her chest into her neck. "Let's not," she said, squishing herself into her seat and fixing her gaze out the window.

"You're attracted to me, *sì*?"

She sealed her lips, silently letting him know he couldn't make her talk.

Nevertheless, he had her trapped and demonstrated his patience with an unhurried sip of his own drink and a brief glance at the face of his phone.

"You smiled at me one day," he said absently. "The way a woman does when she is inviting a man to speak to her."

And he hadn't bothered to.

"I play a game with a friend back home," she muttered. "It's silly. Man Wars. We send each other photos of attractive men. That's all it was," she lied. "If it makes you feel objectified, well, you have a glimpse into how I feel right now."

Her insides were churning like a cement mixer.

"You're embarrassed by how strong the attraction is," he deduced after watching her a moment. He sounded amused.

Her stomach cramped with self-consciousness. Could her face get any hotter?

"This releasing of compromising photos is very shrewd," he said in an abrupt shift. His tone suggested it was an item in political news, not a gross defilement of her personal self. His finger rested across his lips in contemplation.

"Jensen has very cleverly made himself appear a victim," he said. "The moment we accuse him of wrongdoing, he'll claim he only took advice from you and Fabrizio. Fabrizio may eventually implicate him, trying to save his own skin, but Jensen has this excellent diversion. He can say you came on to him, maybe that you were working with Fabrizio, that you sent those photos to ruin his marriage. Perhaps they were cooked up by the two of you to blackmail him into skimming funds. Whatever story he comes up with, it will point all the scandal back to you and Fabrizio and the bank."

"I'm aware that my life is over, thanks," she bit out.

"Nothing is over," he said with a cold-blooded smile. "Jensen landed a punch, but I will hit back. Hard. If he and Fabrizio were in fact using you, you must also want to set things straight? You'll help me make it clear you had zero romantic interest in Jensen."

"How?" she choked out, wondering what was in his drink that he thought he could accomplish that.

"By going public with our own affair."

Gwyn pinched her wrist.

Vittorio noted the movement and his mouth twitched.

She shook her head, instinctively refusing his suggestion while searching for a fresh flash of anger. Outrage was giving her the strength to keep from crying, but his proposition came across as so offhanded and hurtful, so cavalier when she couldn't deny she was weirdly infatuated with him, it smashed through her defenses and smacked down her confidence.

"I don't *have* affairs," she insisted. She looked out the window at the rust-red rooftops below. The houses below were short, the high-rises in the center of the city gone, green spaces more abundant. They were over outlying areas, well out of Milan. *Damn it.*

She wanted to magically transport back to Charleston and the room where she had stayed during her mother's short marriage to Henry. She wanted to go back in time to when her mother was still alive.

"It's such a pathetically male and sexist response to say that sleeping together would solve anything. To suggest I do it to save my job—no, *your* job—"

She was barely able to speak, stunned, ears ringing. Her eyes and throat burned. "It's so insulting I don't have words," she managed, voice thinning as the worst day of her life grew even uglier.

"Did I say we'd sleep together? You're projecting. No, I'm saying we must appear to."

Oh, wonderful. He *wasn't* coming on to her. Why did she care either way?

"It would still make it look like I'm sleeping my way to the top," she muttered, flashing him a glance, but quickly jerking her attention back to the window, not wanting him to see how deeply this jabbed at her deepest insecurities.

From the moment she'd developed earlier than her friends, she'd been struggling to be seen as brains, not breasts. A lot of her adolescent friends had been fair weather, pulling Gwyn into their social circles because she brought boys with her, but eventually becoming annoyed that she got all the male attention and cutting her loose. The workplace had been another trial, learning to cope with sexual harassment and jealousy from her female coworkers, realizing this was one reason why her mother had changed jobs so often.

Her mom had been a runner. Gwyn tried to stay and fight. It was the reason she had stuck it out in school despite the cost. Training for a real profession had seemed the best way to be taken seriously. Yet here she was, being pinned up as a sex object in the locker room of the internet, set up by men who believed she lacked the brains to see when people were committing crimes under her nose.

And the solution to this predicament was to sleep with her boss? Or appear to? What kind of world was this?

She looked around, but there was nowhere to go. She might as well have been trapped in a prison cell with Vittorio.

He swore under his breath and withdrew her phone from his shirt pocket, scowling at it. "This thing is exploding." His frown deepened as he looked at whatever notification was showing up against her Lock screen. "Who is Travis?"

His tone chilled to below freezing and his handsome features twisted with harsh judgment. She could practically see the derisive label in a bubble over his head.

"My stepbrother," she said haughtily, holding out her hand, not nearly as undaunted as she tried to appear. Her intestines knotted further as she saw that she'd missed four calls and several texts from Travis, along with some from old schoolmates and several from former coworkers in Charleston.

All the texts were along the lines of, *Is it really you? Call me. I just saw the news. They're saying...*

Nausea roiled in her. She clicked to darken the screen.

Travis had been vaguely amused with her concern over not having every skill listed in this job posting for Milan. *Do you know why men get pro-*

moted over women? Because they don't worry about meeting all the criteria. Fake it 'til you make it, had been his advice.

Really great advice, considering what such a bold move had got her into, she thought dourly.

But his laconic opinion had been the most personable he'd ever been around her. He was never rude, just distant. He never reached out to her, only responded if she texted him first. He didn't know that she'd overheard him shortly before her mother's wedding to his father, when he'd cautioned Henry against tying himself to a woman without any assets. *There are social climbers and there are predators.*

Henry had defended them and Gwyn had walked away hating Travis, but not really blaming him. Had their situations been reversed, she would have cautioned her mother herself. It had still fueled her need to be self-reliant in every way.

She had been so proud to tell Travis she'd landed this job, believing she'd been recognized for her education, qualifications and grit. *Ha.*

"I guess we can assume the photos have crossed the Atlantic," she muttered, cringing anew.

It was afternoon here. Travis would be starting his day in Charleston, and the fact that he'd learned so quickly of the photos told her exactly how broadly these things were being distributed. Maybe reporters had tracked down the family connection and were harassing him and Henry?

Damn that Kevin Jensen. His headline name was turning her into a punch line.

She set her phone on the table, unable to think of anything to say except *I'm sorry*, and that was far too inadequate.

She swallowed back hopelessness, realizing a door had just closed on her. She could go back to America, but she couldn't take this mess to Henry's doorstep. He'd been too good to her to repay him like that. Travis might make her cut off ties for good.

"You're not going to call him?" Vittorio asked.

"I don't know what to say," she admitted.

"Tell him you're safe at least."

"Am I?" she scoffed, meeting his gaze long enough for his own to slice through her like a blade, as if he could see all the way inside her to where she squirmed.

And where she held a hot ember of yearning for his good opinion.

"He's not worried," she dismissed, feeling hollow as she said it. "We're not close like that. He just wants to know what's going on." So he could perform damage control on his side.

She had worked so hard to keep Travis from seeing her as a hanger-on, so he wouldn't think she was only spending time with his elderly father in hopes of getting money out of him and possibly cut her off. She was vigilant about paying her own way, refusing to take money unless it was a little birthday cash which she invariably spent on groceries, cooking a big enough dinner to fill her stepfather's freezer with single-serve leftovers. She always invited Travis to join them if she was planning to see Henry, never wanting him to think she was going behind his back.

Now whatever progress she'd made in earning Travis's respect would be up in smoke. But what did that matter when apparently no one else would have any for her after this?

"Do you have other family you should contact?" Vittorio asked.

"No," she murmured. Her mother, a woman without any formal training of any kind, had married an American and wound up losing her husband two years into her emigration to his country. He'd been in the service, an only child with elderly parents already living in a retirement home. They had died before Gwyn had been old enough to ask about them.

With no home or family to go back to in Wales, her mother, Winnifred, had struggled along as a single mom, often working in retail or housekeeping at hotels, occasionally serving for catering companies. She'd taken anything to make ends meet, never deliberately making Gwyn feel like an encumbrance, but Gwyn was smart enough to know that she had been.

That's why Gwyn was so determined to prove to Travis her attachment to Henry was purely emotional. It was deeply emotional. Henry was the only family she had.

"You do make an easy target, don't you? A single

woman of no resources or support," Vittorio commented. Perhaps even desperate, she could hear him speculating.

"You must think so, offering an affair when I'm at my lowest," she said. "You might as well hang around bus stations looking for teenaged runaways."

Something flashed in his gaze, ugly and hard and dangerous, but he leaned forward onto the table between them and smiled without humor.

"It's not an offer. Until I say otherwise, you're my lover. I'm a very powerful man, Gwyn. One who is livid on your behalf and willing to go on the offensive to reinstate your honor."

His words, the intense way he looked at her, snagged inside her heart and pulled, yanking her toward a desire to believe what he was saying.

"You mean the bank's behalf. To reinstate the bank's honor," she said, as much to remind herself as to mock him. Her prison-cell analogy had been wrong. This was the lion's cage she was trapped in with the king of beasts flicking his tail as he watched her.

"You understand me," he said with a nod of approval. "We've been very discreet about our relationship, given that you work for us," he continued in a casual tone, sitting back and taking his ease. "But I assure you, I'm intensely possessive. And very influential. This crime against you—" the *bank* "—won't go unpunished."

He was talking like it was real. Like they were

actually going forward with this pretense. Like they were really having an affair.

She choked on a disbelieving laugh, pointing out, "That just switches out one scandal for another. It doesn't change anything. I still look like a slut."

She might have thought he didn't care, he remained so unmoving. But sparks flew in the hammered bronze of his irises, as if he waged a knife fight on the inside.

He still sounded infinitely patronizing when he spoke.

"Sex scandals have a very short lifespan in this country. A little one like a boss-employee thing, between two single adults?" He made a noise and dismissed it with a flick of his fingers. "Old news in a matter of days. I would rather weather that than have the bank suspected of corruption. The impact of something like that goes on indefinitely."

"Do you even care if I'm innocent? All you really want is to protect the bank, isn't it?" She looked at where she'd unconsciously torn off the whites of two fingernails, picking with agitation at them.

"Of course the bank is my priority. It's a *bank*. One that not only employs thousands, but influences the world economy. Our foundation is trust or we have nothing. So yes, I intend to protect it. The benefit to you could be exoneration—which I would think you would pursue whether you're guilty or not. We'll imply that Paolo knew of our affair and that's how he and I were made aware of Jensen's activities. We kept you in place to build the case."

"Will I keep my job?" she asked, as if she was bargaining when they both knew her position was so weak she was lucky she wasn't being questioned by the police right now. Or being hurled from this stupid helicopter.

"No," he said flatly. "Even if you prove to be innocent, putting you back on our payroll would muddy the waters."

"Let's pretend for a minute that I'm as innocent as I say I am," she said with deep sarcasm. "All I get out of this, out of being targeted by *your* client with naked photos that will exist in the public eye for the rest of my life, is a clean police record. I still lose my job and any chance of a career in the field I've been aiming at for years. *Thanks.*"

He didn't own the patent on derision. She found enough scorn to coat the walls of this floating lounge, then turned her dry, stinging eyes to the window.

After a long moment, he said, "If you are innocent, you won't be left with nothing. Let me put it another way. Cooperate with me and I'll personally ensure you're compensated as befits the end result."

"You're going to pay me to lie?" she challenged, her tone edging toward wild. "And what happens when that comes out? I still look like an opportunist."

He didn't flinch, only curled his lip as he asked, "Which lie is closer to the truth, Gwyn? That you want to sleep with Kevin Jensen? Or that you've been sleeping with me?"

Could he see inside her thoughts? Did he know what she fantasized about as she drifted into slumber every night? She sincerely hoped not. Talk about dirty images!

Blushing hotly all over, she crushed the fingers of one hand in the grip of the other, trying to keep herself from ruining any more of her manicure. Having him aware of her attraction made this worse, just as she had suspected. It was mortifying to be this transparent around him.

All she had to do was picture Nadine's disapproving face to know how far protesting with the truth would get her, though. If she had more time, she might have come up with a better solution, but the helicopter was much lower now, seeming to aim for a stretch of green lawn next to a lakeside villa.

On the table before her, her phone vibrated with yet another message.

It didn't matter who it was from. Everyone she knew was being told she had sent naked photos of herself to a married man. The existence of the photos was bad enough, but she was prepared to do just about anything, as the people in Nadine's line of work would say, to change the narrative. Vittorio said this would cut the scandal down to a few short days and she had to agree that it was a more palatable lie than the one Kevin Jensen had put forth.

"Fine," she muttered, swallowing misgivings. "I'll

pretend we were having an affair. Pretend," she repeated. "I'm not sleeping with you."

He smiled like he knew better.

CHAPTER FOUR

HE LET HER into the house, then watched her wander it as he made a call, allowing her to listen as he greeted someone with a warm, *"Cara. Come stai?"*

Gwyn took it like a punch in the stomach, wondering how crazy she was to agree that he could call *her* his lover if he already had one.

The restored mansion was unbelievable, she noted as she clung to her own elbows and stared at the view of Lake Como that started just below the windows off the breakfast nook. The rest of the interior was warmly welcoming, with a spacious kitchen and May sunshine that poured through the tall windows and glanced off the gleaming floors with golden promise. Family snapshots of children and gray-haired relatives and the handsome owner and his wife adorned the walls, making this a very personal sanctuary.

This felt like a place where nothing bad ever happened. That's what home was supposed to be, wasn't it? A refuge?

Would she ever build such a thing for herself, she wondered?

Gwyn moved into the lounge and lowered into a wingback chair, listening to the richness of Vittorio's voice, but not bothering to translate his Italian, aching to let waves of self-pity erode her composure. She felt more abandoned today than even the day her mother had died. At least then she'd had Henry. And a life to carry on with. A career. Something to keep her moving forward. Now…

She stared at her empty hands. Vittorio had even stolen her phone again, scowling at its constant buzz before powering it down and pocketing it.

She hadn't argued, still in a kind of denial, but she was facing facts now. She had no one. Nothing.

In the other room, Vittorio concluded with, *"Ciao, bella,"* and his footsteps approached.

He checked briefly when he saw her, then came forward to offer the square of white linen that was still faintly damp and stained with her mascara.

So gallant. While she felt like some kind of sullied lowlife.

She rejected it and him by looking away.

"No tears? That doesn't speak of innocence, *mia bella*," he jeered softly.

She never cried in front of people. Even at the funeral, she'd been the stalwart organizer, waiting for privacy before allowing grief to overwhelm her.

"Is that all it would take to convince you?" she said with an equal mixture of gentle mockery. "Would you hold me if I did?" She lifted her chin to let him see her disdain.

"Of course," he said, making her heart leap in a mixture of alarm and yearning. "No man who calls himself a man allows a woman to cry alone."

"Some of us prefer it," she choked out, even though there was a huge, weak part of her that wanted to wallow in whatever consolation he might offer. She'd had boyfriends. She knew that a man's embrace could create a sense of harbor.

But it was temporary. And Vittorio was not extending real sanctuary. They were allied enemies at best.

He wasn't even attracted to her. He thought she was a criminal and a slut.

"Just show me where I can sleep." She was overdue for hugging a pillow and bellyaching into it.

His silence made her look up.

"Paolo is still tied up questioning Fabrizio. His wife has very kindly offered her wardrobe." He waved toward the stairs. "She has excellent taste. Let's find something appropriate."

"For?" She glanced down at her business suit, which was a bit creased, but in surprisingly good shape despite her colossal besmirching.

"Our first public appearance," he replied in an overly patient tone, like he was explaining things to a child.

"You said we just had to wait out the scandal for a few days." A strange new panic began creeping into her, coming from a source she couldn't identify.

"Oh, no, *cara*," he said with a patronizing shake of

his head. "I said that the worst of the scandal should pass in a few days. We are locked into our lie for a few weeks at least. You don't get seasick, do you? The wind might come up this evening and the dinner cruise could get rocky."

Vito wondered sometimes, when his dispassionate, ruthless streak arose this strongly, whether his father's genes were poking through the Donatelli discipline he had so carefully nurtured to contain it.

The mafiosi were known for their loyalty to family, he reasoned. The ferocity of his allegiance to Paolo and the bank had its seeds in his DNA. Of course he would do everything and anything to protect both. Of course he would do whatever was necessary to neutralize the threat Jensen posed.

Vito was aware of something deeper going on inside him, though. A pitiless determination to *crush* Jensen. It was positively primeval and he wasn't comfortable with it.

He glanced across at the fuel for his suppressed rage and was impacted by intense carnal desire.

Why?

Oh, Gwyn was beautiful. He couldn't deny it, even though she was pale beneath a light layer of makeup. It had been expertly applied by Lauren's very trustworthy stylist from Como. Like anyone who worked for society's high-level players, the stylist knew any sort of indiscretion meant a loss of more than just one lucrative client. Lauren had sent the woman "to help a friend." The stylist kept her finger on the pulse of celebrity gossip. She had recognized Gwyn with a very subtle start, then grinned and put her at ease so Gwyn had been smiling as she emerged as a butterfly from the chrysalis of a guest bedroom an hour later.

Her smile had faded when she had found Vito waiting for her. That had bothered him, making him feel a small kick of guilt, like he was responsible for her unhappiness.

...targeted by your *client with naked photos that will exist in the public eye for the rest of my life...*

He had asked her for the name of the spa and had ordered a team to look into it, wondering if a connection to Jensen might turn up beyond his wife recommending Gwyn visit it for physiotherapy.

Gwyn could have used something to relax her in that moment, as she'd stood so stiffly, projecting hostility as she seemed to wait out his judgment on her appearance.

He could hardly breathe looking at her. She was a vision in a long, sparkling blue skirt with a high slit and a black, equally glittering halter top that clung lovingly to the swells of her ample breasts. Her midriff was bare and her hair loose so her face was squarely framed by the blunt cut across her brow and the straight fall of rich, mahogany brown. She wore silver hoop earrings and a dozen thin bangles supplied by the stylist. Lauren's shoes were a half size too big, but Gwyn's toes were freshly painted a passionate red.

"You're stunning," he had told her sincerely.

Her hands had grown white where she clutched a small black pocketbook. Averting her face, she'd said, "Not sure why I bothered when people are going to look through what I'm wearing."

"Do you need me to tell you you're beautiful either way?"

She flinched. "Took a long look, did you?"

So much resentment. It annoyed him to be lumped in with all the other voyeurs. He had spent the past hour taking stock of how thoroughly Jensen was arrowing those images back at the bank, how the world media was exploiting Gwyn's naked body for ratings. He had looked at everything *but* her photographs, deliberately sparing her one more pair of male eyes and himself the disturbing dual reaction of arousal and fury.

The thought that men around the world were licking their lips in lascivious heat over her figure was making him grow murderously affronted.

So he didn't appreciate her goading him.

"They're imprinted on my mind," he said without apology, watching something tense and disturbed flash across her expression before she quelled it. "You have nothing to be ashamed of. I don't mean that from a physical standpoint, but that's true, as well."

She reacted with a startled stare of confused vulnerability.

"That sounds almost kind. Are you practicing? Because there's no one here to overhear you being nice to me." Her mouth pouted in consternation, lips possibly trembling a moment before she firmed them.

It struck him that she didn't know he was attracted to her.

He would have laughed if he hadn't been so stunned. Admiration of her figure was a given. Why did she think she'd been chosen for this particular form of exploitation?

But there was more. Tendrils of possessiveness had rooted in him during those first seconds of viewing her pale nudity. A prowling hunger was growing, urging him to make her aware that he ached to touch her. He wanted to see the knowledge, the catch of excitement in her gaze. The exponential increase of passion as it reflected back and forth between them like parallel mirrors.

He didn't know how he knew it would be like that, he just did.

"You'll have to get used to looking insipidly pleased by my compliments," he said to disguise his growing need, grasping at her remark about practicing. "And welcome my touch," he added, giving in to temptation and letting the backs of his fingers graze the softness of her bare arm.

Goose bumps immediately rose on her skin and her nipples tightened.

It was such a visceral reaction he experienced an answering pull in his groin, one that very nearly had him throwing in the towel on his precious discipline. He had wanted to scoop her up and head straight to the nearest bedroom. Hell, the floor.

She blushed. Hard. Hurt flashed across her expression. “I’m already a powerless game piece. Don’t make it worse by taunting me with my own stupid reaction to you.” Shame darkened her eyes, but she dared to threaten him. “Or we will have a very ugly public breakup.”

“And a very hot and public reunion,” he responded fiercely, catching at the taut tendons in her wrists where she clenched her hands into fists. Tucking them behind her back, he pulled her in close and slid his lips along her perfumed neck, eyes almost rolling back into his skull as male hunger slammed through him. He *wanted* her. “Because your reaction to me is exactly what will sell this story of ours. So get used to revealing it.”

Then, because she strained her face away from him, he sucked a tiny love bite onto her neck where it met her shoulder. Her whole body shuddered and a sensual moan escaped her. Her hips bucked to press her mons against his straining erection and lingered to rock with muted need, teasing both of them.

In that second, they could have both lost it, but he had forced himself to release her, his grip on his control far too tenuous for his liking.

He was unsurprised by the hatred she flashed at

him as she took a staggering step away from him. She looked stricken. Shocked by her own reaction. He was unnerved himself. They would tear the skin from each other's bones if they gave in to this thing between them.

That hatred was good, though. It armed him against making love to her. He was driven, not despicable.

She hadn't spoken to him again, moving to the car like an airman with jump orders, sitting stiffly, keeping her stoic expression averted.

Everything in him itched to knock through that wall of hostility with another sample of their amazing chemistry, but he needed time to get hold of himself first.

The driver slowed to a crawl behind the line releasing rock stars, socialites, minor royalty and major league players onto the red carpet.

Vito wasn't on the list, but he knew the American actor hosting the cruise, so he had seized the opportunity to "come out" with Gwyn here. It was a precursor to an international film festival. The guest list was not only small and exclusive, but worldly enough that leaked sex tapes and mug shots were dismissed as "publicity." Nude photos were barely worth mentioning, as common to a portfolio as head shots.

He heard Gwyn's breath switch to measured hisses as she tried to control an attack of nerves. As the car stopped, he took her limp, clammy hand in his—and experienced a thrill of excitement from the contact despite the terror in the gaze she flashed at him.

"Chin up," he reminded her with a patronizing smile, sensing that kindness in this moment would be her downfall. She seemed to find her strength in anger, so he provoked it.

She said something under her breath that wasn't very ladylike, making him want to smile, but that wouldn't do for their purposes.

"Let them know how much you hate them," he said as the door beside him opened. He stood, bringing Gwyn with him, not giving her a chance to chicken out. Then he paused, giving the paparazzi the moment they needed to realize who they had.

The girl from the photos.

With Vittorio Donatelli.

His hand possessively slid so he had his arm around her and drew her closer, dipping his chin to look into her withdrawn expression with just the right level of concern before he lifted a hostile, contemptuous glare to the wall of cameras, silently messaging Kevin Jensen that he had messed with the wrong man's woman.

A buzz of gasps went through the crowd and the bursts of light intensified into a wall of exploding lights. The shouts became a rabid din.

Gwyn swallowed and revealed the barest moment of anguish before she leveled her shoulders and sent a haughty, dismissive glance toward the cameras that was gloriously effective in its disparagement. Her upward glance at Vito was not only a cold, silent demand that he remove her from this place, but a wonderful expression of trust that he would and could save her from it. He doubted she realized how revealing it was, but he saw it, knew the cameras caught it and was deeply satisfied.

She kept her spine iron straight beneath his hand as he steered her through the blinding lights to where the purser stood at the top of the steps to the gated marina.

"I'm not on the list," Vittorio told the uniformed young man. "But I'm on the list."

The purser didn't even relay his name, only glanced at the wild reaction they'd provoked and recognized the value they added to the event. "Thank you, sir. Enjoy your evening."

Vittorio started toward the steps, then turned back. "If Kevin Jensen is on the list, he's not on the list. Understand?"

"Absolutely." The purser nodded and flipped a page, striking through a name.

This morning, life had been normal.

Somehow, in roughly twelve hours, Gwyn had gone from mousy banking representative to notorious internet sensation. Thanks to Vittorio secluding her today, the full reality of her situation hadn't hit her until that moment outside the limo. Then strangers had called her name, clamoring for her to turn, shouting disgustingly invasive questions in a dozen languages.

When did you pose for those nude photos?

How did Mrs. Jensen find out about your affair?

Is Vittorio Donatelli your lover?

She stepped onto the yacht and a murmur rippled through the crowd. Heads tipped together and a few people pointed.

She instinctively edged closer to her date and his fingertips dug into her hip, oddly reassuring.

The last thing she ought to count on Vittorio for was protection. He'd behaved like a bastard earlier, using her own reaction against her like that. She was sick with herself for rubbing into his groin like she ached for his penetration—which she did. She was even sicker that finding him hard had excited her to the point she would have let him have her right there at the top of the stairs if he'd wanted.

Men were simple creatures, she reminded herself. Comedians were always complaining about erections popping up like dandelions at inconvenient times. As much as it would soothe her ego to believe Vittorio was attracted to her, she knew he couldn't possibly feel the same lust that had cut into her like a knife. His reaction had been about as personal as shivering from the cold.

They were united in one thing: pretending they were in a sexual relationship to defuse Jensen's allegations.

So she slithered closer to him, ignoring the fact

that she drew genuine comfort from his strength. If he stiffened in a kind of surprise before tightening his arm around her, well, she wasn't a masochist who wanted another mean-spirited lesson in how incapable she was of resisting him. She stood close; she didn't soften and invite.

"Vito!" A gorgeous blonde approached them, tugging a legendary, award-winning, big-screen star in her wake. They turned out to be the host and hostess.

Gwyn silently laughed at herself. If the crowd was goggling at her, she goggled right back. The yacht was full to the gunwales of faces she'd seen in movies and on TV. Hugely famous people. It added a fresh layer of surreal to her already bizarro day.

"Thank you for coming," the tall, stunning supermodel said in a New York accent, kissing Vittorio on the mouth. "We'll have so much more exposure for the premiere now. I didn't see the photos," she said to Gwyn with an offhand shrug. "But my agent represents five of the top underwear models in the world. Judging from your figure, he would love to be your first call if you want to make lemonade out of this. Don't put it off. Attention like this doesn't last. Vito has my number."

"Vito," Gwyn repeated a moment later, when they were alone.

"My friends and family call me that. You should, too."

"Should I call her agent, is the real question," Gwyn said, taking a deeper drink of her champagne than was probably wise, but the impulse to get legless drunk was very strong.

"I would prefer you didn't," he said in a tone that was oddly lethal.

"Call her agent? Why? What other kind of work can I get? Even Nadine thought I wasn't good enough at my job to earn *this* promotion without falling onto my back. Maybe it's time I gave in to what the world has told me all my life and allow myself to be objectified. Make money on God's gift." She waved down her front.

An arc of dangerous fire flashed in his gaze again. "Have you come up against a lot of sexism in your life?"

"Is there an amount that's reasonable and acceptable?"

They were approached by someone else, stealing her moment of possibly taking him aback. They spent the next hour mingling. It wasn't awful, but she was tongue-tied and Vito kept stealing her champagne, setting the flutes out of her reach and giving her sparkling water or fruit juice in exchange.

"If you don't let me drink," she said at one point, fake smile pinned to her face, "people are going to think I'm pregnant. Surely I've hit the redline on scandal for one day?"

"I'm letting you drink. I'm just not letting you get drunk. You'll thank me tomorrow."

"I highly doubt you'll ever hear those words out of these lips," she assured him.

"We'll see," he said, catching at the hand she reached to the passing tray and tugging her in the opposite direction. "Come."

"Where?"

He only drew her from the main deck where glass panels provided a windbreak, keeping the laughing, dancing crowd contained in a pool of colorful light off a rotating mirror ball. A musician who had risen to fame three decades ago was going strong, shredding the piano, playing with a band of indie rockers on guitars and drums.

Vito tugged her down a narrow flight of stairs to where a cool gust raced along the lower deck, making her cross her arms as the chill hit her in the face.

"It did get windy," she said, hanging back in the alcove at the bottom of the stairs.

He removed his taupe linen jacket and draped it over her shoulders, enveloping her in a scent that was both his and something else. His cousin's aftershave, maybe, because he'd also raided the closets in the master bedroom. "We have work to do, now that you've relaxed."

"What kind?"

He drew her toward the stern where foam kicked up in a widening trail behind the yacht. The rush of wind and churning water filled the air. Pinprick lights from distant houses danced against the black silhouettes of the mountain-backed shoreline.

And a handful of smaller boats paced this big

one, bouncing on its wake, buzzing like mosquitos. Something flashed. A camera.

"Oh."

"Sì," he confirmed. "We are stealing a kiss, *mia bella*."

"You can try," she said stiffly, turning her head to glare at him with antagonism, hands on the rail. "I've about had it with being robbed of things I'm not willing to give up. This cruise could get very rough indeed."

He leaned his back into the rail and set his feet wide, then indicated she should come into the space. "I'm offering a kiss," he cajoled, surprising her with his tender tone. "Would it be such a chore for you to accept it?"

A spasm of pain went through her, increasing when she saw another flash and suspected her moment of torment had just been caught and would be fed to the online trolls.

She found herself ducking her head, letting him draw her into his chest in an embrace that she knew he staged to look tender, but it *felt* tender. Like a place of shelter. She was on her very last nerve and desperately wanted to believe she was safe with him, but she couldn't. Not by a long shot.

"I don't kiss strangers," she muttered into his chest.

He smoothed her hair behind her ear and his breath warmed her cheek as he spoke. "We're lovers, *mia bella*."

In her periphery, more flashes were sparking, but

maybe that was the electric reaction he provoked in her.

"You don't even find me attractive. Can you imagine how it feels to kiss someone you know feels nothing for you? Actually it's worse than that. You feel contempt. This is not a nice place to be. I can't pretend to be okay with it."

His hands stilled on her. "Have you had many lovers, Gwyn? You keep surprising me with what sounds like naivety."

"How is it naive to know that all these seduction moves of yours are motivated by a desire to protect the bank, that you're actually overcoming disgust to touch me?" She lifted her face to glare at him, unable to read his face in the dark. "Are you going to tell me next that I'm being too cynical?" She nearly choked on her own words. She was growing weak just standing against his body heat, reacting to him even though she knew he felt nothing toward her. This was so unequal.

"You're a very beautiful woman. You must know that." He rested the heel of his hand on her shoulder, fingertips toying at her nape beneath the fall of her hair.

The caress was so beguiling, the words so throaty, her whole body responded. Her knees weakened, her skin tightened and her nipples prickled. Deep between her thighs, damp heat gathered. Her breath hitched.

At the same time she heard the levelness in his

tone and understood that his body might be growing hard, but his mind was still not affected.

"I suppose this *is* an affair then," she said, feeling him give a small start of surprise.

"What do you mean?"

"Well, it's not a relationship with a future. It's going to serve a purpose then end with neither of us calling or texting. You're right. I haven't had a lot of lovers and they've mostly been hit and runs. That's why I don't date much. I hate the part when I'm left feeling used. That's why I don't want to kiss you right now. I'll just feel dirty after."

"Ah, *cara*, you are very naive," he said with a gentle laugh. "You're in a position to use *me*. Stop being so nice and do it. You'll feel terrific."

She gave him her profile, staring into the dark, angry that he made being nice sound like a character flaw. Angry that her life had been destroyed. Angry that there was no substance to what was going on between them. She was an object. Nothing real or important. This was how her mother had felt all the time.

A self-destructive impulse rose and she tossed her hair as she looked up at him.

"Fine. We'll kiss."

It was too dark to tell whether his brief hesitation was surprise or something else, but his hand moved to cup her cheek and he bent, capturing her mouth in a firm, hungry possession without a lead-up. No delay.

Because they were lovers, she reminded herself as excitement tore through her veins. According to the illusion they were projecting, they were familiar enough with each other to throw themselves into a passionate kiss without preamble.

Heart pounding, she returned his kiss with all the emotions roiling in her. Fury, mostly. She let her hand go to the short hairs at the back of his neck and increased the pressure, drawing him down to her, hurting herself with the way she mashed her mouth against his, liable to leave both of them bruised as she scraped her teeth against his lips in punishment for all that he'd done to her. For all that the world was doing to her.

He grunted and his hand went low on her back, pressing into her bottom to pull her tighter into him, fingertips flagrantly tracing the line between her cheeks.

She didn't protest. She shuffled closer, shoving herself aggressively into his frame, like they were combatants. She moved her hand to take a fistful of his hair, hoping his scalp stung while she moved her lips under his, mouth burning with avid, angry friction.

With another gruff noise, he lifted his head, let her catch one breath, then closed his arms more tightly around her, swooping into a deep, dominant kiss, tongue spearing boldly into her mouth.

Her reaction might have been frightening to her if she wasn't so close to exploding. She needed this outlet, this contained space of banded arms keeping her from flying apart. She fought letting him take over as long as she could, flicking at his tongue with hers, trying to make him break, but he was too strong willed. Way stronger than her.

With a little sob, she finally capitulated, softening and letting him take control.

Her reward was a wash of delirious pleasure. Suddenly she felt what this kiss was doing to her. Her blood was hot, her erogenous zones sensitized and singing. His body seemed to envelop hers in sexual need. She was so steeped in desire, her knees folded.

She would have gone anywhere with him in that moment. Would have let him do anything. She wanted him to cover her and push inside her and take her to a place where nothing could touch her.

His assertiveness eased. His hand moved soothingly over her back. His damp lips tenderly caressed hers until they broke apart to gasp for air. He tucked her head under his jaw and held her ear against his pounding heart.

She rested there, trying to catch her breath, listening to his heart slam, feeling like she'd been running and now the ache of exertion was catching up to her.

He was hard, she realized, and she panged again with longing for this to be real, for them to make love so she could lose herself in mindless pleasure. She ought to find his desire threatening, she thought. Or offensive maybe. She didn't move away from pressing against him, though, liking that evidence of his reaction even if it was strictly physiological. She stayed in that little cave of safety his arms provided, face pressed to his shirt, body sheltered from the wind by his broader one.

And she started to cry.

There was no stopping it this time. It wasn't a grand storm, just a slow leak of tears that grew into a steady, unstoppable flow. Her control surrendered to exhaustion, like a drowning victim letting go and sinking beneath the surface. She clung with limp arms and leaned her weight into him as pulsing waves of suffering rocked her.

He didn't tell her to *shush*. He held her, rubbed her back and didn't say a word.

CHAPTER FIVE

VITO SAT IN the armchair of the hotel room, feet on the ottoman, wearing only his pants. He was pretending to read emails, but sat angled so he could watch Gwyn sleep.

A full-out rainstorm had manifested while she'd been fixing her face in the head, after their kiss. The yacht had raced to moor at the nearest marina and, while most of the guests scrambled through sheets of rain for taxis to take them to their hotels, he had walked into the yacht club and paid a fortune for a top-floor room. He hadn't been interested in leading the paparazzi back to the mansion and Gwyn had been at the end of her rope.

He could have taken a suite, he supposed, but he didn't want anyone counting how many beds had been slept in. He had shared this one with her—until he'd given up trying to sleep. She'd been emotionally drained and slightly drunk, looking disturbingly vulnerable and wary after she'd washed her face and put on his shirt to sleep in it. She had threaded her bare legs under the covers and kept firmly to her side of the bed.

He'd kept his pants on, since he never wore shorts, and tried not to touch her once he had put out the lights and crawled in beside her. At least until he'd realized she was curled into a ball, shivering from the chill of getting soaked by the rain. He could have risen to turn off the air-conditioning, but he'd spooned her instead.

When she had stiffened, he'd said, "Go to sleep," in the same quietly firm tone he would use on any of his abundant underage cousins, nieces and nephews who might creep down the stairs when they ought to be in bed. Molding Gwyn to him, he'd gone quietly out of his mind while she had relaxed into the hot curve of his chest and thighs.

She had dropped into a deep sleep, leaving him nursing an aching erection, blood burning like acid in his arteries. Every time he dozed, his mind took him back to kissing her on the deck, when she'd aggressively tested his control.

He didn't know how he'd kept from lifting her skirt. Possessiveness, perhaps, because in that moment he hadn't cared if anyone saw his naked ass, but the idea of the paparazzi catching another glimpse of her unclothed had been intolerable.

He'd tried to slow things down while he calculated whether to steal into a stateroom or ask for one to be assigned, so they wouldn't risk interruption.

She had started to cry.

This woman. He was trying very hard to vilify her, to help maintain some distance, but there was no question in him any longer as to whether she had posed for those photos. She was too devastated to be anything less than violated.

Which did things to him. Provoked something that could turn into a blind savagery if he dwelt too much on the injustice.

He sipped the coffee he'd made in the small pot, studying her timeless features, so well suited to her surroundings.

The building was classic Renaissance, imposing and symmetrical. The interior was equally ornate and gracefully proportioned, enriched with dark wood grains and gold accents upon fervent reds and royal blues. The setting made a beautiful foil for her pale skin, pink lips and long dark lashes.

He'd neglected to close the heavy curtains so sunlight poured across her cleanly-washed face. The collar of his white shirt was turned up against her cheek, the unbuttoned sleeve pushed far up her bare arm.

His Lover At Rest, he thought with a sardonic smile, toying with the idea of snapping her photo. His conscience stopped him. *If it makes you feel objectified, well, you have a glimpse into how I feel right now.*

He wasn't bothered by her taking a photo of his photo. He knew he was good-looking. Female attention had always been abundant in his life in the very best way. He wasn't surprised that she found him attractive and certainly wasn't offended by it. He liked it. Too much.

She wasn't as comfortable with their chemistry. She was feeling used and he was being a bastard, not letting her see that he was equally ensnared by lust, but wanting her was weakness enough. Letting her see it would be akin to handing over a weapon, something he was too innately self-protective to ever do.

His phone vibrated in his hand and he dragged his attention off her peaceful expression to see that his cousin was forwarding something.

Can you deal with this? Will talk more when I get there. Leaving in a few hours.

Vito understood by Paolo's desire for a face-to-face that he was being abundantly cautious with traceable, hackable things like texts and emails, but it surprised him that Paolo was coming to Como. He had been working from home, refusing to leave his wife's side as she approached the end of her third pregnancy.

But his cousin was smart enough to see the implication behind Vito's appearance with Gwyn last night. He would want more details, to be sure they had their story straight, especially before he made further statements to the press.

The multitude of demands for more information from all corners was threatening to break Vito's phone, coming from every direction from family to news contacts to the bank's core investors. The story across the sea of media had shifted from lurid curiosity about the woman in the photos to deeper speculation as to who she was and how she had ensnared not just one, but two powerful men into a nude photo scandal. Was she sleeping with both of them?

He stroked his thumb along the edge of his screen, deciding it was time to feed another tidbit to the press, leading them away from Jensen's version of events toward his own.

Yesterday, he had ordered a team to look for a connection between the spa owner and Jensen, suspecting it could be a laundry for some of the funds Jensen had funneled. Even if the spa's only crime was the breach of Gwyn's privacy, he didn't see any reason they should remain open and making money while Gwyn suffered.

With enormous satisfaction, he touched the query from one of his former paramours who worked as an anchor for an Italian morning talk show. Quote me as stating that the photos were taken without her consent at a local spa, he messaged to her.

As the *whoosh* sounded to tell him the text was sent, he could practically hear her spiked heels racing down to her producer's office, intent on identifying said spa and surprising the owner with an early-morning interview. She would seize world coverage with her exclusive by noon.

With a smirk at how easily the press was played,

he turned his attention to the email Paolo had forwarded.

It was from Travis Sanders, director of an architectural firm Vito had never heard of. A quick swipe to his browser revealed it was a growing global corporation based in Charleston. Henry Sanders had started in real estate and morphed into renovation and restoration. His son, Travis, had earned his degree then took over his father's firm, expanding into design and engineering. All of their projects were prestigious; the most current one was a cathedral in Brazil.

Vito read Travis's email to Paolo:

I haven't heard from my sister since the tenth of last month. If you're screening her calls, stop screening me. I want to hear from her.

Short and decidedly acrid.

Gwyn shifted on the bed, rolling onto her back and opening her eyes. Confusion quickly fell into a wince of memory. She glanced at the empty spot beside her, sat up, saw him and brought the edge of the sheet up to the buttons closed across her chest.

"I thought you said he was your stepbrother?" Vito said.

"Who? Travis?" She frowned in sleepy confusion. "He is. Why?"

"He wants to hear from you. He thinks we're preventing you from calling."

She sighed and looked at the landline beside the bed like it was a snake he'd asked her to pick up.

Since she'd left her own mobile back at the house, he rose and took his across to her. "Would you rather text?"

Her gaze flickered across his bare chest and wariness trembled in her eyelashes while sexual awareness brought a light pink glow to her skin. He would have smiled with satisfaction if his entire body hadn't tightened in response. Her scent was coming off those rumpled sheets in a way that tugged at his vitals.

She expertly sent off a quick message and handed back the phone, not looking at him.

Despite it being very early in Charleston, the phone vibrated immediately with a response.

Vito glanced at it and couldn't help a dry smirk. "He wants to know his father's birthday. To confirm that was actually you who just texted, I imagine."

"Seriously?" She took back the phone, tapped out a lengthy message and slapped it back into Vito's hand.

He glanced at the exchange, reading that she'd told her stepbrother she was fine, not being held hostage, didn't know what to say and hoped the press wasn't bothering Henry. She wanted Travis to apologize to him for her.

Vito frowned at her expression of misery, started to tell her what was in store for the spa, but another message came through.

"'This isn't like you,'" Vito read.

"How the hell does he know what I'm like?" she muttered, sliding her feet out the side of the bed. "He barely talks to me."

"You're to call him when you can talk freely," he read aloud as she headed toward the bathroom.

She made a noise and said, "I'm going to see if it's possible to drown in a shower."

"Don't take too long. I'm hungry and plan to order breakfast now that you're up."

Funny how something as simple as a shower became a saving grace in a time of crisis. Washing her hair, smoothing a soapy facecloth over her body… It was comfortingly normal. Routine. She took her time, thinking of nothing as water rained down upon her.

Until her mind drifted to hearing the shower in the night.

Why had Vito risen to shower at 2:00 a.m.? He'd been hard against her butt. She remembered that. If she hadn't been so drained, she might have turned and let him do something she would be regretting right now.

Had he touched himself in here? Pleasured himself?

When he could have had her out there?

The thought struck like a blow, tightening her midsection, making her miserable all over again. She had to stop thinking there was any sort of potential between them. Maybe sex was an option. He'd told her to go ahead and use him, after all. But that's all it would be: empty sex. There was no room for romance. They weren't lovers. Despite appearances, they weren't dating. They weren't even friends.

This was all fake.

And her life was a complete disaster, she confronted anew as she stepped from the shower and faced a choice between last night's sparkling evening wear and his rumpled white shirt. She was not in a fit mental state to start any kind of relationship.

She pulled on the robe from the back of the door. It had an embroidered sailboat on the left lapel and was made of thick, comforting chenille. She knotted the belt and emerged to scents of ham and eggs, coffee and sweet pastries. Her stomach contracted. When had she last eaten, she wondered? Vito had forced a few morsels on her last night from the extravagant buffet, but she hadn't been interested.

He was closing the door behind someone as she came out and waved at a stack of clothing that had been delivered. "See if that fits."

She didn't know what to say and found herself fingering through the clothes. There was a clean shirt for him, a short-sleeved, collared one in cobalt blue along with clean socks.

For her, he'd ordered clean underpants, a camisole with a shelf bra in butter yellow, palazzo pants with a subtle floral print and a sheer top that picked up the colors in the pants with splashes of emerald and streaks of pink.

"We're going shopping so you won't have to wear it long if you don't like it," he said, making her realize she was frowning.

"No, it's fine. I thought I'd be wearing the robe back to the house." She looked for price tags, didn't find any and started to worry. How would she pay for this?

"Let's eat," he said, indicating the set table before the now open window.

Their view looked onto the red umbrella tables six stories below, the marina of bobbing, million-dollar boats and the deceptively placid lake glinting in the cradle of mountain peaks.

"Is the shopping really necessary?" she asked, breaking the yoke of her poached egg with the tine of her fork.

He shrugged. "It's a parade for the cameras and you need clothes for all the circulating we'll be doing over the next few weeks, so, yes. I would say it is."

She watched her fork tremble as a fresh wave of helpless anger swamped her.

"I would like to remind you that I don't have a job. How am I supposed to pay for a new wardrobe?"

"You are so cute, Gwyn," he said, *so* patronizing. "I am indulging my *innamorata*. It's what besotted men do."

Her appetite died. She put down her fork, vainly wishing she wasn't sitting here naked under a robe he had funded. She wished she had a better choice than walking out of here in clothes that were borrowed or an outfit chosen and paid for by him. She wasn't used to being this powerless. Even when Travis had been unknowingly annihilating her sense of self-worth, she'd had a job and enough savings to get herself and her mother started over in a cheap room if Henry had called off the wedding.

"Women love shopping, Gwyn. Why are you so upset by the prospect?" Vito asked, tucking into his breakfast with gusto.

"Because this isn't like me," she said, tartly quoting her stepbrother. "My mother didn't have much. She made ends meet, but we lived very simply and I still do."

She typically ate scrambled eggs she cooked for herself, not delicately poached orbs on toasted ciabatta with garlic and a pesto hollandaise, garnished with shallots and plum tomatoes. She drank orange juice she mixed from concentrate, or instant coffee, not mimosas and rich, dark espresso that made her want to moan in ecstasy with the first taste.

She swallowed her tentative sip of the hot, bitter brew and set down her tiny cup, noting that Vito was watching her, like he was deciding whether to believe her. She hesitated to open up, but figured it was better to be honest about her background than to hide it.

"Mom met my stepfather while working as a janitor in his office. Travis was *not* impressed by his father's choice in second wives. He was at university and I moved into his old room for my last year of high school. I guess it was weird for him to suddenly have this geeky girl underfoot whenever he visited his dad. Strangers living in his house."

She had taken refuge in homework when Travis was around, only emerging to eat dinner where Henry had put her at ease and made her laugh.

"My mother genuinely loved his father," she said, silently willing Vito to believe her. "She never would have brought me into any man's home for any reason except to give me a father. I think of Henry that way." She had to drop her gaze as she admitted, "But the day before their wedding, I overheard Travis warning Henry that we might be gold diggers. I thought his mind would change over time, as he saw that we were just trying to be a family, but a year into their marriage my mother was diagnosed with cancer. I was supposed to move out, go to college, but instead I stayed to help Henry nurse her. I took some online courses, but Mom felt like such a burden on us. Travis didn't come around much. I know how it looked to him, like Henry was stuck with a pile of medical bills for someone he shouldn't have to support."

She stared into the harsh glare of sunlight on the water to sear back the tears gathering in her eyes.

"It was such a raw deal that she finally found a man who loved her, who wanted to take care of her, and she died before she could make a proper life with him. Make him happy."

"I'm sorry to hear that," Vito said, sounding sincere, covering her hand.

She removed her hand, forcing herself to shrug off the bleak sadness.

"I'm very conscious of the fact that Travis thinks I'm only maintaining a relationship with Henry because he has money and I don't. I never take any when he offers, so letting you swan me in and out of Italian boutiques is not exactly the picture I want to paint so my stepbrother will let me continue visiting the only father I've ever had."

She looked at him, blinking several times to bring her vision back from a wall of white to see his toughened yet brutally handsome expression.

"But I'm hardly in a position to demand the luxury of pride, am I?" she added caustically.

He was watching her with a gravity that made her feel naked all over again. "Would he really stop you from seeing him?" he asked.

She shrugged. "I don't know," she muttered. "He loves his father as much as I do and wants to protect him. He wasn't trying to be cruel. I mean, you'd probably say the same thing to your own father in that situation, wouldn't you?"

Vito's stare was inscrutable. He held her gaze for a long time, like he had a million responses and was sifting for the best one. He settled on saying, "Eat," and lowered his attention to his plate.

Well, that settled that, didn't it, she thought facetiously, and forced herself to take a bite.

* * *

No matter how sincere Gwyn seemed, Vito couldn't afford to let himself be swayed emotionally. While she finished getting ready, he reviewed her background more thoroughly.

She interrupted, emerging from the bathroom with a more natural look that was infinitely more beautiful than last night's smoky eyes and sharp cheekbones and red, glossy lips painted by the stylist. Gwyn had frowned when he'd handed her the pots of color and paint, grumbling about not wanting to look like a ghost if she was going to be photographed. If not for that, she implied, she wouldn't have accepted the makeup at all.

"What do we do with last night's clothes?" She looked for them.

"I've made arrangements."

She stared at him.

He lifted his brow in inquiry.

"I borrowed something. I want to be sure it's returned in good condition," she said.

"It will be." He frowned, annoyed by what sounded like a lack of faith, but also seeing yet more evidence of the do-it-myself streak of independence she seemed to have. "I reviewed your file and some other details," he told her as they left the room.

She looked over her shoulder at him, dismayed, but not fearful. "Like?"

Her financial situation. Her debt level was low, but she had a little, and hadn't made any significant payments or purchases recently. There had been nothing to red flag her as possessing or spending a sum that might have been embezzled. Instead, he'd found more evidence that she was exactly as she portrayed herself.

"You've worked hard for the education and position you've attained," he acknowledged once they were in the privacy of the elevator. "But Fabrizio signed off on your transfer despite there being two candidates with more experience. It supports what you said yesterday, that you might have been recruited because you were green and possibly more likely to let things slide out of ignorance."

"So you're willing to believe it based on your own assessment of hard evidence, but nothing I say has any bearing. My word means nothing to you. Isn't that the story of every woman's life." She shrugged on the cloak of righteous anger she'd been wearing since he met her, but he could sense the hurt beneath.

He wasn't sure what kind of reaction he expected, but he hadn't expected that. His belief in her *meant* something to her. It made him realize exactly how much power he had over her and he wasn't sure he was comfortable with it.

Since when did he not embrace power? He loved it!

But he was suddenly confronted with how vulnerable she was. To all the men in her life, but especially to him, right now. It slapped at his conscience, made him think again about her saying he would protect his father. The joke was on her. His real mother had been light-years ahead of his father in social status, belonging to the Donatelli banking clan. His father had been on the bottom of society's spectrum. A criminal of the vilest order.

He had cold-bloodedly seduced her with an eye to his own gain.

What are you *doing, Vito?* he chided himself.

He was protecting the bank, he reminded himself. And his blood was decidedly hot when Gwyn's hand was in his own.

He strolled her through the late morning sun, ignoring the cameras, entering every boutique on the promenade and refusing to leave without making a purchase.

But for a woman who only needed to act enamored to get herself out of trouble, she did a lousy job of it. She wasn't outright defiant. No, her resistance was subtle enough to give credence to what she had said earlier about not wanting to look like a gold digger. She needed cajoling to enter a change room, pulled a face at the prices and frowned at the growing number of bags he was having sent back to the yacht club.

It was beyond his experience. Every woman he knew enjoyed being spoiled this way, whether sisters, mother or lovers. He had been raised to be chivalrous, and not only owned a sizable number of shares in the bank, but investing was his living. He made more money in a day than he could spend in a week. This was pocket change.

He began taking special care, looking for items that were particularly flattering to her, complimenting her, trying to soften that spine and coax a smile of pleasure out of her. Why couldn't she relax and see the fun in this?

A motorcycle jacket with a faux fur collar and narrow sleeves that capped the tops of her hands to her knuckles looked genuinely delightful on her. He stood behind her as she eyed it in the mirror.

"It suits you. Makes you look as tough as you are," he said.

She met his gaze in the mirror. "You do this a lot, don't you? I honestly didn't see you as the kind of guy who had to buy his women."

She might as well have butted that hard head of hers back into his lip and nose. He tightened his hands on her shoulders to freeze her in place.

Her gaze met his again and she saw the danger there, stilling, hand on the zipper of the jacket.

"Be very careful what you say to me, *cara.*"

"You want those vultures out there to believe this," she said with a small toss of her head to the front of the store, where music was blaring so loudly they could barely hear each other even back here. "I don't have to. Or does your ego demand that I fall for you for real?"

Once again she had him thinking about a powerful man exploiting a vulnerable young woman.

That wasn't what this was.

She moved the zipper an inch then shrugged his hands off her shoulders. "Buy it if you think I should have it. I don't care."

The hell of it was, he believed her.

Gwyn watched cute sundresses and silk scarves, two hats and a designer bag that cost the earth all go into colorful boutique bags. Vito told her they'd buy evening gowns in Milan—for what?—but insisted she get trendy jeans, cocktail skirts and flirty tops, lingerie that she flatly refused to let him watch her try on and shoes. Dear Lord, the shoes.

Deep in her most covetous, most materialistic heart, she adored Italian-made shoes. She'd been saving up for a pair, browsing regularly as she debated whether to be practical and buy something she might wear often or ridiculously capricious and own something that would sit in a box in her closet, to be worn on only a few special occasions.

Vito bought her six pairs of very chic, very expensive day shoes and completely dismissed them as, "They'll do for now." More, he assured her, would be purchased with the gowns in the city.

She might have protested, but he was already angry with her. That moment at the mirror had made her tremble inside, he'd looked so lethal. At the same time, she knew he wouldn't hurt her physically. It was her heart, her own ego and self-confidence that were in peril.

Especially because, despite her nastiness, he didn't let up on his solicitude. They walked from store to store and paparazzi swarmed around them, clicking and flashing and capturing every murmur and expression. One called something particularly disgusting and she flinched.

"Ignore them," Vito growled, drawing her closer to the shelter of his big body, brushing his lips against the tip of her ear as he spoke, then smoothed his fingers through the tails of her loose hair, caressing her waist, so attentive to her needs.

She imagined she looked deeply smitten every time he touched her like this. That's why she'd had to insult him and drive a wedge between them. Her response to his pretend seduction was dangerously real. Her nipples tightened when all he did was touch the small of her back. She flushed with desire when she inhaled the scent of his neck.

How was she so comfortable under his touch? That's what she wanted to know. Normally she was quite standoffish with men. If they so much as took her elbow while they walked her down the street, she found the presumptiveness of it annoying.

Not Vito. Her skin called out for each light graze of contact. She was in a perpetual state of readiness, skin sensitized and aching with anticipation, eager for his merest caress. She wanted him to smother her with his big body. Absorb her.

In some ways it was exhausting. She was incredibly relieved when he pointed to a car with a chauffeur in sunglasses leaning against it, reading his phone. "We'll take a drive to some viewpoints, see if we can lose these cameras before we head back to the house."

Their last two boutique bags went into the trunk where the myriad of other purchases were now arranged along with dry cleaner bags holding the clothing they'd worn last night. The man really was a demigod, taking care of the dreary details of life with what seemed like a magical snap of his finger and thumb. Forget the other conquests who fell for this routine. She was becoming one of them. How could any woman *not* find this level of provision seductive?

She settled with a sigh on the leather seat in the back, pretending she wasn't aware of the scooters that kept buzzing up beside them for the next ten minutes as they drove into the hills. The windows were blacked out, however, so the followers soon fell away, accepting that their opportunity was over and they might as well go file the photos they had and collect their payments.

The car climbed high above the lake, the twists in the road taking them into stretches of quiet thoroughfare, where she finally let out her breath in a sigh.

Vito leaned forward to close the privacy window and poured both of them a water from the bottle in the door.

"Was it so bad?" he asked. "Spending my money?"

"No," she said, adding a sarcastic, "How was it for you?"

She heard how suggestive that sounded and made a noise into her glass.

"Why does everything I say come out sounding dirty around you?" she muttered.

"Freudian slip?" he suggested.

She slid her thumb along the rim of her glass, blushing and saying nothing.

"Your silence speaks volumes," he taunted.

"Am I the first woman to find you attractive? I doubt it," she said caustically.

"You're the first to be so annoyed by it," he said with a hint of laughter in his voice. "Why? Because you're so tempted?"

"I've never been a drug user and that's what it would be," she muttered. "You're sitting there like a giant painkiller promising to keep me from feeling the bus that's crushing me. So, yes, I'm tempted." She couldn't believe how honest she was being. It wasn't like her to be this blunt, but what shred of dignity was left to lose? "But I've never gone to bed with a man purely for physical release. It makes me feel cheap to consider it."

"You're incredibly insulting when you want to be, aren't you? The problem, I think, is that you don't know how powerful this particular painkiller will be." He leaned across and set her glass in her door. His was gone and his hands went to her waist. "Come here."

"What—?"

He dragged her to straddle his thighs, making her

stiffen in surprise at the sudden intimacy of having her legs open across him, her inner thighs lightly stretched by the press of his thick, hard ones.

She kept her arms stiff, holding herself off him, but she was intrigued despite her wariness. "There's no one to see this performance," she reminded tautly.

"Yes, I know," he said smokily, and stroked his hands up and down her thighs, massaging in a way that sent ripples of anticipation into her pelvis. With a little shift, he slouched and they were sex to sex, her tingling loins firmly seated against the very hard ridge of his erection.

"If only I still worked for you and could charge you with sexual harassment," she said, but her voice had thinned and her twitching thighs wouldn't cooperate enough to lift her away.

"I don't have to buy women, *cara*. They come to me for this." His hips came up just enough to press where too many nerve endings were centered. She bucked in an allover response, gasping.

"You're so full of yourself," she told him, shivering, not fighting the hands that pressed her hips so she felt that delicious grind again.

The corners of his mouth deepened in satisfied amusement. "Let's see which one of us wants to be full of me, hmm?" His hand slid up her side, across her shoulder to cup the side of her neck.

A trail of tingles followed his caress, sensitizing her, making her go still when self-preservation instincts told her to get the hell off his lap.

As he exerted a tiny pressure, urging her forward, asking for her mouth against his, she gave in.

It's only a kiss. They'd done it before.

But this wasn't a kiss. It was a match to a flame.

As her mouth reached his, he captured her in a hungry kiss, like last night, only hotter. With a confident hand on her butt, he rocked her against his erection, making her shudder and take over the move herself, seeking the rhythm that would build the desire in the heated, dampening flesh between her legs.

Distantly she told herself to be cautious, remember this was about the bank. He was only doing this to prove a point, but her arms went around his neck in a kind of instinctive twine. She pressed to crush her breasts against his chest. Their tongues tangled and they both opened their mouths to deepen the kiss into something flagrant and wildly passionate.

Maybe there was something else she ought to have been thinking about, fretting over, but few thoughts of any clarity stuck after that. She became a being of pure sensation. All her awareness centered on the points where they touched, how he stroked her back and hips, how her body prickled and responded like firecrackers were exploding at different points.

His hand slid to cup her breast, weighing and gently massaging. She rubbed her nipple into his palm, never so free when it came to sex. Maybe if he'd seemed surprised by her lack of inhibition, she would have pulled back, but he groaned with appreciation, encouraging her, giving her all the pressure she needed as he shaped and squeezed her breast. She loved the way the light fabric of her top and silky cami made it easy for him to find and tantalize her nipple, pinching the peak and causing a stab of arousal straight between her legs.

She gasped and moaned approval. More heat rushed to pool in her loins, making her ache there and seek that hard ridge. She rubbed, trying to soothe the needy throb between her legs, unable to remember the last time she'd had any sex, let alone thrown herself into it like this. No man had ever aroused her this quickly and thoroughly with little more than a kiss and a few brazen caresses.

She arched as his other hand found its way beneath her top and pulled her cami askew, so he could pull back and look at her through the translucent film of her overtop. They both watched his thumb circle her nipple, flicking back and forth, stimulating the tight bead so she shuddered and panted, scalp tight, excited beyond what she could imagine could happen from such a simple bit of teasing.

"Come here," he said, urging her to lift on her knees and push her nipple toward his mouth.

She did, bracing her hands on his shoulders, vaguely aware they were in a moving car. Maybe the blur around them was empty of humans, but the darkened glass at her back wasn't. She ought to be showing more decorum, but his tongue moved the silk of her top against her nipple in delicate friction. The dampness of his mouth enclosed her in heat, sucking and inciting. She was lost, groaning with delight as he tortured her, licking and moving that damp fabric, squeezing the swell of her breast just enough to push more blood into the tip.

She was going to climax from this alone, she thought, working her nails with agitation against his shirt, thinking she should stop this, but she was compelled to keep going because it felt so damned good.

Her waistband released and his other hand slid in, confident and possessive, cupping soaked lace, saying something in Italian she didn't have the wherewithal to interpret, but he sounded pleased. Like he was complimenting her. She absolutely flowered when he sounded so appreciative and admiring.

He held his palm steady for her to grind herself into the heel of his hand. She moaned with pleasure as her arousal became acute. She tore at his collar and tried to stroke his skin, wanted to bend and kiss him, but as she pulled back, he stared at her chest.

"Give me the other one," he growled, eyeing her left breast, still tucked away.

With trembling hands, she lifted her top out of the way, pushed the cami down so her breasts were thrusting out the top of it, brazen in the extreme—

He opened his mouth wide on her bare nipple and she nearly screamed at the sensation of his teeth closing softly, dragging all the way to the tip before he sucked her into the deep, wet cavern of heat that was his greedy mouth.

A rush of need flooded into her sex. Into his palm.

He made an animalistic noise and his fingers pushed past silk, fingertips seeking, two penetrating, burying deep, thumb tracing and finding. Circling.

"Yes," she gasped, giving herself up to the stunning height of pleasure, welcoming the thrust of his fingers, clasping him hard to her breast as he nipped in a way that was just short of pain. The sensations he was offering were so sharp and intense it was almost too much to bear. She clenched, trying to hold back, realizing how close she was to losing it. This wasn't what she'd meant to happen.

His arm clamped around her waist and he kept lashing her with those twin sensations until she couldn't hold back. Orgasm crashed over her. Her body nearly buckled under the power of it. Her cries of abandon filled the backseat and she pressed her hands to the ceiling, all of herself offered to him as he pleasured her, nearly bursting into jagged tears at the intensity of her release. Dying. She was dying and would never breathe again.

The paroxysm held her for a long time, until she slowly became aware that his caress had become soothing.

His damp hand moved, sliding onto her hip then cupping her backside, urging her to nestle her tender, throbbing flesh against the aggressive ridge of his erection straining the front of his pants. He lifted his head and licked at her panting mouth, teasing her into kissing him back.

She was still shaking with reaction and kept her eyes closed as she kissed him with swollen, trembling lips, aware of his hardness everywhere: shoulders, arms, thighs. Even his lips were firm where hers were soft with spent pleasure. His heart was pounding while she was still trying to catch her breath, both of them damp with perspiration.

Finally she dragged her eyes open to see he had a very smug, satisfied light in his half-closed eyes. That arrogance was unnerving, making her realize he had completely taken her apart while losing none of his own control. Only his collar was slightly askew, his hair barely out of place.

He told her in a low growl what he wanted to do to her.

What was wrong with her that she responded with an internal clench of anticipation to his dirty talk?

She pushed off his lap and shakily tidied her clothes, avoiding his gaze, trying not to think of where his hand had been. How she'd sounded as she called out with release. Had the driver heard her? How did things just keep getting more mortifying?

She managed to rally, responding to what he'd said with a scathing, "The way you're looking so self-satisfied, I'd think we already did that."

He angled to look at her, reaching to smooth a wisp of her hair from its tangle on her eyelashes. Her pulse leaped with excitement, but his finger didn't even brush her skin.

"It was bothering me that other men had seen you

naked. But no man has ever seen you like that, have they? I'm very satisfied."

What an egotistical—

"You're a jerk," she told him, thinking there were saltier words and she was tempted to find them.

"Are you losing the feel-good already? Because I'm right here, ready and willing to take you to your happy place all over again."

"Oh, shut up," she snapped, turning her face to the window. Pride. Who knew it was such an unaffordable luxury?

CHAPTER SIX

GWYN DIDN'T KNOW how close she'd just come to being taken in the backseat under the straying eye of his driver. Oh, Carlo would have known they were petting, would have turned up the music so he wouldn't hear anything indelicate, but neither he nor Gwyn knew that Vito had nearly lost control, so caught up in Gwyn's pleasure he'd almost found his own, fully clothed and completely at her service. He'd barely stopped himself from rolling her beneath him on the seat, stripping them bare and quite possibly planting a baby in her without a single thought for the consequences.

The thought disturbed him. Was that how he'd been conceived? In a fit of blind passion that completely disregarded the impact to the woman in question?

By the few accounts Vito had from his adoptive parents, his mother had been deeply infatuated, if far too young and naive for a thirtysomething gangster with a pitiless determination to get whatever he wanted. He had wanted Antoinietta Donatelli. He had seduced her. His family had always sworn up, down and sideways that Vito wasn't a product of rape. No, he was the product of a man taking advantage of a woman who didn't have nearly the worldliness needed to resist him.

Not unlike Gwyn, who didn't take lovers strictly for the pleasure of physical release.

Because, he suspected, no man had given her a release like that. He probably shouldn't have, but her animosity had been eating at him. That remark about buying women and her resistance toward him on every level had been grinding away at his control. When she had called herself "cheap" for wanting to sleep with him, something feral in him had snapped, demanding that he *show* her how good they would be together.

Cheap? It was unique and precious, beyond even what he had imagined it could be. Disconcertingly powerful.

And honest.

Her reaction now, so taken aback by her own abandonment, told him how thoroughly he had owned her in those moments. He thrilled to it, but it caused a shift inside him. Something he wasn't fully prepared to examine, fearing he was making a rationalization to justify getting what he wanted: her.

But the way she'd ignited in his arms made thinking of anything except possessing her impossible.

* * *

They seemed to have left the paparazzi far behind and circled back toward the house. As soon as they were inside, Gwyn went straight through to the small patio outside the back door, where the cool afternoon breeze off the water gave her the first proper breath she'd taken since coming apart at Vito's touch.

She went down the steps to the pool deck where she stared out over the lake, blood cooling, hands curled around the rail to ground her back into harsh reality. Why had she let that happen? And what did it mean for the rest of this pantomime they were acting? Would they become lovers in every way, not just a one-sided grope that only proved his superiority over her?

That was the part that devastated her. She could give herself orgasms if she wanted them. But despite all the ways he'd turned out to be different from the urbane Italian gentleman she'd fantasized about, she was even more in thrall than ever. Would she become his lover?

She couldn't imagine finding the will to say, *No.*

Vito came outside with two wineglasses and a corked bottle. He wordlessly poured and offered her one, not speaking until she took hers.

"Salute," he said, gaze trying to catch hers.

She couldn't do it, too aware of how intimate things had been between them. Too vulnerable to him.

"I keep making you angry because it seems the

only way to keep you from falling into despair," he said, as though explaining the answer to a riddle.

"Something else for my own good?" She snapped her gaze up to his.

He smiled faintly. "Whatever works."

She released a shaken sigh, finding his statement not exactly comforting, but oddly bolstering. He wasn't toying with her for fun, but trying to help her in his backhanded way.

She couldn't deny that his lovemaking had, for a few minutes, completely wiped away her anxiety over her nightmare of a life. Now everything was flooding back and she would be very thankful if he did something annoying. Despair hovered like a rain cloud looking to move in and burst over her.

He set his glass on a table and shrugged out of his new jacket, a vintage cut in light wool with leather patches at the shoulders. It was gorgeous on him, very debonair, but the dove-colored shirt beneath was equally smart, clinging to his muscled shoulders, buttons open in a V that showed his throat and collarbone and a few dark chest hairs.

He slung the jacket negligently over the back of the nearest chair, attention shifting to his phone. With a flick of his thumb across the screen, he paraphrased from something he was reading. "The spa is claiming they had no knowledge of the photos, but the press has found the same connection my team discovered this morning. Your masseuse is related to one of Jensen's employees. I'll take you to lodge a formal complaint with the police when we return to Milan so they can look at pressing charges for invasion of privacy."

"Charging the masseuse doesn't put the blame on Kevin, though, does it?"

"He has worked very hard to keep his hands clean, but we'll get there. It's early days yet." He picked up his glass and sipped, continuing to read his emails.

Days. It hadn't even been two full ones, but she'd already gone further with him than most of the men she'd dated for months. She was in so much trouble if that was a precursor of what was to come.

Pensively sipping the pale gold of the wine, she wound up exclaiming a very sincere, "Oh, that's very good!"

Not that she was any sort of connoisseur, but Travis always brought wine when she cooked and he didn't punish anyone with cheap stuff. She'd been enjoying trying bottles here in Italy and hadn't found a bad one, but this surpassed anything in her price range.

Vito glanced up, offering what looked like a very genuine smile for a change. "It's the private reserve from my great-grandparents' vineyard. One of my cousins runs it and doles the bottles out to family every year. We could make a fortune, but it's too good to sell."

"Do you—" Gwyn forgot what she was going to ask as a flash of movement caught her eye.

Was that a little boy? He touched his lips to signal her to keep quiet as he climbed the rail that bordered the pool terrace then darted behind an oversize terra-cotta planter.

Vito followed her gaze and glanced backward at the empty landscape, then brought his alert frown back to her. "What's wrong?"

She started to say, "I saw a little boy—"

Before she could get the words out, the boy was barreling straight for Vito's legs.

In the same moment, Vito's expression hardened. He plunked his glass down and spun in a fluid motion, like he knew exactly what was coming. He crouched, grabbed, then threw the boy high into the air as he straightened, then caught him firmly and held him nose to nose.

"You little gremlin. I ought to throw *you* into the pool."

"Do it!" The boy's laughing eyes brightened with excitement. He splayed out his arms and legs, ready to fly through the air into the still, blue water despite being fully dressed.

"I won't," Vito told him, hitching the boy's wiry figure onto his arm so they were eye to eye. "That's your punishment for trying to push me in. No swimming at all. Say hello to Miss Ellis," he said, indicating her with a nod. "This is Roberto. He has all of his mother's sass and twice his father's disregard for danger."

"I was going to come in with you," the boy excused, curling his arm around Vito's neck and pressing his cheek to Vito's with open trust and affection. He was speaking perfect English but could have been Vito's son, his looks were so patently Italian. He turned his attention to Gwyn and pronounced what sounded like a coached speech. "It's nice to meet you. Welcome to our home." He offered his small hand for a shake, making it a firm one.

"It's a beautiful home," Gwyn said, ridiculously charmed, even though he couldn't have been more than five. "I'm very pleased to meet you, too."

Roberto gave her a stare reminiscent of Vito's most delving look.

"Are you American? Mama is Canadian and sometimes people think she's American, but your accent is different. You sound like our housekeeper in Charleston."

"Good ear," Gwyn said with a bemused smile. Honestly, he had more sophistication than some thirty-year-old executives she had met.

"Did you drive here yourself? Where is your father?" Vito asked, giving the boy a little bounce.

"He won't let me drive," Roberto said with a disgruntled scowl, then pointed to the top floor. "He's putting Bianca in her bed. She fell asleep in the car. She has a cold."

"He brought both of you? How is your mother?"

"So pregnant," a woman said, coming out the back door of the house.

Lauren Donatelli was very pregnant, but carried it beautifully on her tall frame, glowing and graceful as she came down the short flight of steps onto the pool terrace, nary a waddle in her step.

Gwyn recognized her from photos she'd seen in the Charleston news several years ago, along with the odd image published in the company newsletter where Lauren invariably stood next to Paolo looking warm and approachable despite how aloof and distant her husband always seemed.

"Hi, I'm Lauren," she said, offering her hand.

"Gwyn," she murmured, and tried to thank her for the loan of clothes, but was waved off.

"Anything for Vito. Hello, *caro*," she said to him. He stooped a little so she could kiss both his cheeks.

"Should you be anywhere but a maternity ward?" he asked her.

"I offered to check myself into a clinic, but the doctor said there was no point since it will be at least two weeks. Paolo wouldn't let me stay in the city without him, of course. His mother is at the house, but you know what he's like. Won't let me out of his sight." She shook her head in exasperation.

"Roberto was born inside their front door. Bianca delivered in a car," Vito informed Gwyn.

"It was easier to lose the paparazzi waiting at the gate if we made it look like we were going for a simple family outing," Paolo said, arriving with a baby monitor that he set on the table next to Vito's wineglass. "Miss Ellis," he greeted with a cool nod.

"Signor Donatelli," she murmured, intimidated to the soles of her feet.

Thankfully his son pleaded, "May I swim, Papa. *Per favore?*"

"Vito and I must talk about work, but if you put on your trunks you can come to the shore with us and wade."

"Yes!" Roberto dropped out of Vito's arms and started to run toward the house.

"Quietly," Lauren warned, slowing his step. "Don't wake your sister. I'll start dinner," Lauren said with a well-practiced hostess smile.

"You will not," Paolo told her. "I'll cook when I come in. Stay off your feet."

A man willing to cook. Gwyn was so astonished it took her a moment to blurt out the sensible solution that broke the challenging stare between the married couple.

"I can make dinner."

Everyone looked at her. These two men really were too much masculinity in one impactful wall for any woman to handle.

"Unless you need me to be there while you talk?" She had no doubt she would be the topic of their discussion. Frankly, she was hoping to avoid listening to her humiliation being kicked over like something a dog owner had failed to dispose of properly.

"I would appreciate your cooking, if it's something you don't mind doing," Paolo said, then turned to his wife. "You may sit and chop tomatoes if you promise not to put your weight behind it."

She made a face at him.

"If our daughter wakes, would you call me?" he added to Gwyn. "She's under the weather and will want to be held, but Lauren needs to takc it easy. At this stage the hiccups will start her labor. I have my hands full enough without catching a baby today."

"It's twenty minutes out of your life," Lauren murmured, looking at her fingernails. "I don't know what you're complaining about."

He caught her hand and brought her curled knuckles to his lips. "I can barely think of anything else as it is. You know that. Try to buy us a few more days while we settle this work crisis? Please?"

The looks they were giving each other were such a mix of open emotion, tender and teasing and loving, Gwyn knew she ought to look away. It was a private couple's moment, but it was so beautiful, she was transfixed. She wanted that. The cajole and silent communication and connection that bound in a thousand ways. The secretive smile. The way they looked like they wanted to kiss, but were in no hurry because Paolo was stroking her bent knuckle against his upper lip and they had an abundance of time and opportunities for loving affection.

"Maybe this one will have my patience instead of your lack of impulse control," Lauren teased. "We could get lucky."

"Do not blame me!" Paolo scoffed. "They wind up with your sense of humor and think it's funny—stop laughing. I'm serious. No laughing. You'll put yourself into labor."

Lauren disobeyed, releasing a hearty chuckle that made Gwyn smile along with her.

Their son came outside in his trunks and Gwyn turned her expression of amusement into a greeting for the boy, giving the couple their privacy to exchange a kiss.

When she glanced at Vito, she saw he was watching her, his expression unreadable.

A few minutes later, Gwyn was moving around Lauren's kitchen, chatting with her with surprising ease. Perhaps Lauren wasn't resting with her feet up as her husband had demanded, but since she wasn't holding anything heavier than a paring knife, Gwyn didn't say anything. Besides, every birth story she'd ever heard was a lengthy process, happening in the midnight hours. Lauren wasn't complaining of a backache or any of those other things women talked about as precursors to labor. She was relaxed and pleasant and ever so nice!

Feeling as vilified as she did, Gwyn was deeply relieved to be treated like a normal person.

"Did you get that top at the boutique on the far end of the lake?" Lauren asked. "I bought the red-and-gold one two months ago. They have amazing stuff, don't they?"

Gwyn agreed, then, as she set a pot of water to boil and the conversation lulled, she screwed up her courage and said, "I, um, lived in Charleston before I came here. I'm not trying to pry," she hurried to add. "I just thought I should tell you that I couldn't help but be aware of all the coverage about your husband. Um, first husband, I mean."

Lauren's expression smoothed to something very grave, gaze sliding away to hide her thoughts. "It was a heartbreaking time."

"I'm very sorry for your loss," Gwyn said quickly, feeling it was the decent thing to say to the widow of a war hero, but it wasn't why she'd brought it up. She wasn't asking the big question that had been on everyone else's mind at the time: had Lauren slept with her husband's best friend the night she had learned her husband was dead? The answer to that was outside throwing rocks into the lake, as far as Gwyn could tell.

"I wouldn't have mentioned it except… Is it bad taste to ask how you handled all the attention?" Gwyn asked.

Lauren smiled with empathy. "It's exhausting, isn't it? People so love to judge." She opened a cupboard and drew out a box of linguine noodles. "I guess you make peace with whatever you've done to get yourself into that situation and accept that you can't control what others think or say. It's what you think of yourself that matters."

"I'm obsessed with what other people think," Gwyn admitted glumly. She had a childhood full of starting new schools, being teased for being first to wear a bra, then constantly being underestimated because she was smarter than anyone expected from a girl with good looks.

Her mother had nursed the same sort of angst, having quite an inferiority complex due to an orphan's upbringing. Sometimes Gwyn wondered if that had been her mother's reason for moving so often—part habit, but also a continuous attempt to reinvent herself in hopes of ever-elusive acceptance.

For Gwyn, landing this job in Milan had been her first step in believing she really was good enough and smart enough to earn respect on her own merit, but she was seriously struggling to believe in herself now.

And while she could dismiss the dim views of strangers and comfort herself with the knowledge she hadn't done anything to deserve the humiliation she was suffering, she was acutely sensitive to what Vito might be thinking of her.

Why? Why couldn't she shrug off his judgment of her?

Because he affected her on every level, she acknowledged. Because he had literally controlled how she felt in the car today, working ecstasy through her. If he had the power to make her feel good, he also had the power to devastate her.

She started to blush, feeling the heat rise from deep spaces to become a hot glow on her cheeks. *Such* power. She wished she could get him out from under her skin!

"My turn to pry," Lauren said, handing Gwyn

a bag of mushrooms, scanning Gwyn's guilty pink cheeks with interest. "This thing with you and Vito. Have you really been seeing him? Or is it just for show?"

"What?" Gwyn said dumbly, nerveless fingers nearly losing the featherweight of the bag.

"You don't have to tell me," Lauren said with a teasing twinkle in her eye. "I'm being nosy because he's one of my favorite people, but I realize there are things at the bank that can't be discussed. Believe me, I know." She made a face of long suffering. "But..." She sent Gwyn a cagey look as she moved to the sink. "I have a feeling that if he'd been seeing you before this story broke, I would have known."

"What do you mean?" Gwyn asked, knocked off balance by something she couldn't identify. Was she suggesting Vito acted differently around her? Lauren had only seen them together for a minute and a half before they'd come inside and the men had gone to the beach.

"I don't know. There's something in the way he looked at you—" Lauren shrugged, starting to wash her hands, then cut herself off as she gave the soap dispenser next to the sink a shake. "I think there's a new one in the upstairs bathroom," she said, turning off the tap.

"I'll get it," Gwyn said, setting down the mushroom she was stemming.

"I'll peek in on Bianca while I'm up there," Lauren said with a wave.

Seconds later, Lauren's voice was considerably less relaxed as she swore loud enough for Gwyn to hear her all the way down in the kitchen.

"Are you all right?" Gwyn called, making a panicked start up the stairs.

Lauren came to the open door of the main bathroom, bracing herself against it with a white-knuckled grip, expression somewhere between exasperated and remorseful.

"He's going to kill me. Tell Paolo my water just broke."

Vito was not a romantic, but he had seen the longing in Gwyn's expression and felt a kick of commiseration. Paolo and Lauren made anyone covetous of their happiness. He envied his cousin himself, not just for finding his soul mate, but for his freedom to pursue a life with her. Even if Vito did find the right woman…

He was adept at not letting himself dwell on such things and cut off the thoughts as he and Paolo took Roberto down to the water and exchanged reports.

Paolo expanded on what he'd already messaged, saying Fabrizio was a tough nut, but cracks were showing in his story. The board of Jensen's foundation was not yet moved to worry about any of this, let alone meeting to discuss Jensen's possible removal. Jensen himself was leaving the country for a minor quake that was more photo op than actual disaster relief, but would bolster his image.

"You haven't frozen the foundation's assets?" Vito asked.

"I don't have grounds. I'll be pushing for a forensic audit once Fabrizio breaks or we're able to prove Jensen was behind the instructions to move funds, but he is definitely playing a rough PR game right now. This—" He chucked his chin back toward the house and Gwyn. "I see where you're going and it would work if it was true, but I can't go on record saying that you've been having an affair with her all along. We all may have to testify at some point."

"Sì," Vito agreed. "But you can state that unnamed sources—me—" he shrugged "—made you aware some time ago that there were worrisome transactions within the account. We put it on a watch list and saw no reason to remove Miss Ellis because she was not only conducting herself with sound ethics, but has since proven to be an excellent source of knowledge with regards to the foundation's legitimate activities."

"You're convinced she has been conducting herself ethically?"

It was the judgment Vito had been avoiding making, aware that Gwyn was already a weakness to him. He wanted her and therefore he wanted to believe her, because how could he have an affair with a woman who was committing crimes against the bank? He couldn't gamble his family's future on his own selfish desires.

But at every stage, if she was the type to manipulate a man like Jensen, her actions would have been different, right up to this afternoon in the car. *He* would have been the one losing control to her hand or mouth, he was sure, if she was the type to lie and steal and wish him to believe otherwise.

At no time since he'd met her had Gwyn acted dishonorably, though. In fact, she was trying to protect the little family she had from the fallout of dishonor that, if she was innocent, wasn't hers to bear.

The problem was, if she *was* blameless, he was going to have to kill the man who had done this to her.

"I believe she is Jensen's victim, yes," Vito said, and heard the cruel edge on his tone. "They gambled on her lack of experience and when she showed her intelligence, they threw her to the wolves."

He understood the expression *bloodthirsty* as he said it. His tongue tingled and his throat tried a dry swallow, but he didn't long for water. He craved the tang of suffering for Jensen and Fabrizio and whoever had helped them by taking those photos.

He felt the quick slash of Paolo's glance before he returned his watchful gaze to his son, but his cousin obviously read his mood.

"So we imply you two have been having an affair all along and she's been feeding us information. What happens when I'm asked point-blank if I condone my VP of operations sleeping with a customer service rep?" Paolo folded his arms, eyes on his son, but his tone added, *Because I don't.*

"You never comment on the private lives of your family or your employees," Vito said, which was true. "But as a rule, you expect to be notified of such relationships in a timely manner and you have no quarrel with when and how your VP of operations has advised you of this connection."

Paolo shook his head, mouth pulled into a half smirk. "People call me competitive, but strategy plays are your drug of choice, aren't they?"

"Live the lie and it becomes the truth," he said blithely.

Paolo sobered. "The photos certainly look convincing," he said with another pointed look, before returning his alert attention to his son in the water.

Vito had seen the photos online from today's shopping trip with Gwyn and last night's kiss. The passionate embrace on the stern of the yacht still made his pulse pound just thinking of it. His mind went to the car, the wet heat clenching his fingers as she shuddered and cried out with fulfillment.

There were a million reasons why he should merely *act* like they were an item, rather than make the affair real, but they would make it real. He knew it in the same way that adversaries knew a physical confrontation was coming. They could put it off, because they both knew in their gut that neither of them would come away unscathed, but their making love was inevitable.

"No comment?" Paolo prodded. "Because if she's a victim, don't make her more of one."

That stung. Vito hid it, countering lightly, "What do you want me to say? I like women. I can't help that they like me back."

It was the laissez-faire attitude he always affected when discussing paramours. Paolo was the head of the family. He couldn't escape marriage and the duty of producing progeny. Vito didn't have the same pressure to procreate. He was at liberty to play the field the rest of his life if he wanted to.

Paolo sent him a dour look, the one that told him Vito could show the rest of the world, pretend his entire life was one long, lighthearted affair, but he knew better.

Paolo knew him better than anyone. They had been adversaries themselves in childhood, scrapping constantly. Two strong-willed, alpha-natured boys of similar ages would. It had culminated in a fistfight of epic proportions when they were twelve, not far from here, on the property Vito's family still owned, high in the hills overlooking the lake. They had been beating each other with serious intent, their superficial argument transitioning into a far more serious drive for dominance over the other. Neither was the type to give up. Ever.

Paolo's father had stopped them. He'd been a man of strength and drive and purpose, the conservative head of the bank that had been the family's livelihood for generations. He was a loving man, a devoted uncle, a pillar of strength for all of them.

And he'd nearly cried when he'd pulled the boys apart.

You can't do this, his uncle had said. *No more. You're family.*

Vito didn't like upsetting his favorite uncle, but he had had nameless frustrations swirling inside him. He was claimed to be part of their clan, but he wasn't. Something was off and he knew it. He loved his parents. His mother doted on him. His father showed great pride in every one of Vito's accomplishments, but he didn't feel close to them. He was different. Not quite like them, not the same in temperament or looks as his sisters. He felt more kinship toward Paolo's father than his own. When they all came together for these sorts of big, family occasions, he caught watchful looks from some of the older aunts and uncles. It made him tense. Meanwhile, Paolo was so very confident in his own position, Vito was compelled to knock his cousin out of it.

So the angry accusation had come out. *Am I? Family?*

The way Paolo had looked to his father for that same answer, as if he too suspected Vito was not quite one of them, had been the most devastating blow of all.

Paolo's father had stood there with his hand on his hair, like he'd come across a bomb blast and was suffering a kind of shell shock himself, unable to make sense of the broken landscape.

Then, very decisively, he had nodded. *Fine. I'll tell you. Both of you.*

Vito had never questioned such huge news coming from his uncle, rather than his father. It was a Donatelli matter, after all. *He* was a Donatelli. Legally he was a Donatelli-Gallo. Women kept their maiden name when they married in Italy. He and his sisters used a hyphenated version of their parents' names, but he had always felt more drawn to the Donatelli side of his family and used that name to this day.

Because he had no Gallo in him, he had learned, sitting on a retaining wall overlooking the lake, hearing his uncle explain to him that his mother, his *real* mother, was the youngest Donatelli sibling, Zia Antoinietta. The aunt who had died and was rarely mentioned because her loss made everyone so sad. Vito would later look at her photographs and see more of himself in her than in her older sister, the woman who had called herself his mother all his life.

Your father was a dangerous man, Vito. Dangerous to us as a family, to the bank and very dangerous to your mother. I pulled her away from him so many times, but she kept going back. She was pregnant. She thought she loved him. I'll never forgive myself for not finding a way... She finally realized what was in store for both of you when he knocked her around and put her into labor. She called me to come to her where she was hiding from him. She died having you. I held her, waiting for the damned ambulance, and she begged me to keep you away from him, to keep you from turning into a mafioso like him. He wanted an heir to his empire, but it's a kingdom built on blood and suffering. We would have called you Paolo's brother, but well, you know the story we tell instead.

Vito did. His adoptive mother, the middle sister, often told the story of how she had thought she had miscarried, but Vito had miraculously survived. In reality, she and her husband had spirited her sister's newborn to the family home at the lake and waited out a suitable time before presenting Vito as their son. His birthday was off by four months.

I paid a fortune to the doctors to write out a certificate that you had died with her. And threatened your father with murder charges if the affair ever came out. I'm certain he would come for you if he knew you survived, Paolo's father had warned.

Vito could only imagine the fortune Paolo's father had paid to keep the liaison from becoming public knowledge and destroying the bank as it was. If online scandal rags had existed then, the affair wouldn't have suppressed as easily, he was sure.

Your mother was too precious to me, you are too precious to me, for me to watch you two beating each other senseless. Turning to Paolo, he had lifted his shirt, showing a long scar that had always been blamed on surgery, but not today. *Did I take this knife trying to bring home my sister so my own son could kill hers? Save your strength for the fights that matter, then fight them together. Understand?*

He hadn't had to warn them to keep the secret. That was a given. He had risen and urged Paolo to come with him, to give Vito time alone.

No, Paolo had said. *I'll stay.*

They had sat in silence a long time, the space Paolo's father had taken up a wide gap between them. Finally Paolo had said, *Do you want to punch me?*

Yes, Vito had seethed. But he hadn't. They'd never fought again. They rarely mentioned it. Eventually Vito had learned the name of his biological father and the man's predilection for violence had sickened him. Then there was the second son's equally conscienceless disposition.

Vito wanted to believe he was different, but how could he claim to be a better man than what he'd come from when just the thought of those men and their actions put him into a state of mind willing to crush and kill? Vigilante justice was still brute force and only proved he was more like his biological father than he wanted to admit.

So he couldn't in good conscience make children with a woman without telling her what kind of blood he carried and he couldn't reveal the truth without endangering his family and the bank.

Therefore, he was a confirmed bachelor, destined to have affairs with women who didn't expect a future and to commiserate with the struggles of child-rearing from the sidelines.

"Your lips are blue. Come out," Paolo ordered his son.

"Three more," Roberto said, holding up three quivering fingers, teeth chattering, narrow shoulders shaking as he prepared to dive for yet another colored rock.

"One," Paolo said firmly.

"Two," Roberto responded.

"Everything is a negotiation," Paolo muttered, making Vito set his teeth because Paolo was complaining about a privilege not every man had. "Two. Then—"

"Paolo!" Gwyn came to the rail above them, at the edge of the pool deck. Her eyes were wide, her face pale. "Lauren says her water broke!"

Paolo went white and grim, swearing tightly. "Out, Roberto. Now. Stay with Vito," he ordered his son, locking gazes with Vito long enough to cement the command that Vito keep his son from drowning, but also sharing a moment of genuine fear.

It struck Vito that Paolo had never told Lauren why he didn't find these home births of hers as much of a joke as she did. He knew women could die.

It also told him how volatile his secret still was, if Paolo hadn't shared it with the woman who was his other half.

"I'll call the ambulance," he said to Paolo's back, pulling out his phone as his cousin took the stone stairs in great leaps, already pushing back his sleeves.

CHAPTER SEVEN

"THAT WAS THE most remarkable experience of my life," Gwyn said forty minutes later, as the ambulance carried off a grumbling Lauren and an infant boy who had squawked once, latched perfectly, then fallen asleep snuggled against her.

"They're just going to tell me that everything is fine and I can go home if I want to. I wish you hadn't called them," Lauren scolded Vito on her way out the door.

"Humor us, *mia bella*," Paolo said with equanimity, buttoning his clean shirt with hands that might have tremored a little, but he'd barely broken a sweat while carrying his wife to their bed and catching their son minutes later.

He'd been very coolheaded, calling Gwyn to bring him the bag he'd prepared with clean towels and receiving blankets, speaking to his wife in a calm, tender tone, using sterilized clips and scissors from the bag to cut the cord himself, as if he'd been a midwife all his life.

Their daughter slept through most of it, waking in time to glimpse her new brother, but quite content to cuddle with Vito amidst all the activity. Roberto called the little girl Bambi, which was adorable, and both children stayed with Gwyn and Vito while Paolo went in the ambulance with his wife. A car pulled out from the house across the street where the drivers and other ancillary staff were staying, following to bring them back once Lauren and the baby had been examined.

Vito didn't say anything as he closed the door. In fact, his color was down and he took a measured breath as if he'd just dodged a train.

"You're green around the gills, Vittorio," Gwyn chided, amused. "Were you worried?" She hadn't had time to panic and was riding a high of amazement.

"Lauren makes it look easy," he said in a tone that suggested he was well aware labor and delivery didn't always go so smoothly.

"I'll say," Gwyn responded. "I didn't even get the water boiled!" She moved into the kitchen where she had managed to snap off the gas on her way to fetch Paolo. "Shall I finish making dinner?"

"We'll help," Vito said, sliding Bianca onto a stool while Roberto climbed into the one his mother had been using. Vito was very good with the children and they openly adored him, grinning at his teasing, behaving angelically as he gently kept them on task.

Vito exchanged several texts with Paolo, who

mentioned that everything was fine but there was a small delay in seeing the doctor.

"Paolo will be taking some family time now that the baby is here," Vito said to Gwyn. "We had planned for this, but we'll have a proper meeting when he gets back to review a few things before I assume his duties. You and I will spend the night here and head back to the city in the morning."

Gwyn nodded absently, too caught up in watching him cut up a little girl's food, steady Roberto's hand as he shook out red pepper flakes then smoothly reached to top up Gwyn's wineglass with a practiced flair. Throw in his ability give a woman orgasms and get the laundry done and he was the perfect man in every way.

He met her gaze.

Her thoughts must have reflected in her it. Building a career had been a dominating goal in her life, partly because she'd seen how hard her mother had struggled to support herself without a proper profession. Gwyn had focused on her degree and finding the right job and chasing opportunities for advancement. It had meant relegating a husband and children to a dreamy "someday" that she hoped would find her when the time was right.

But she longed for a place to settle and call home. She wanted a family within it that wasn't a tenuous late-in-life connection, but a network of blood ties like this family had, where a woman could be nosy about a man simply because she cared about him.

She could leave her children with him in utter confidence that he would keep them safe and give them thc affectionate security that fed their souls.

"Be careful, Gwyn," Vittorio said with gentle gravity, holding her gaze.

She scanned for hazards the children might tip before meeting his gaze again, confused.

He wore the tough, circumspect look of the man who'd first stared her down in Nadine Billaud's office.

"This is not our life," he said in the same temperate tone. "Not yours. Not mine. So stop thinking it will happen."

She was far too transparent around him. It was achingly painful to be this obvious, especially when he had touched her so intimately they were practically lovers, then shot down her dreams so dispassionately, leaving her nursing a giant ache that hollowed out her chest.

"Not with you, perhaps," she said, lifting her glass and her chin, holding his gaze even though the locked stare made her stomach cramp. "But there's no reason I can't have something like this, someday. Is there?" she challenged.

He might have flinched, but she wasn't sure.

And the silence went on long enough for her to remember her own notoriety. Would anyone want her after this? Ever?

A noise at the door told them the new parents had returned.

Gwyn rose to set two more places, grateful for a reason to turn away and hide that her eyes were welling up.

"Do you need the address for my flat?" Gwyn asked the driver as they slid into the car the next morning.

"I have it, thank you," the driver assured her as he closed her door for her.

The air was fresh, the sun shining and the children had both hugged her at the door. Nevertheless, Gwyn's good mood took a dip when Vittorio made no protest against her going home.

She wasn't about to ask him what *he* had planned for her, though. She had lain awake a long time last night considering her options. Her life wasn't over, she had concluded. It just needed to be re-envisioned.

As Vito flicked through messages on his tablet, she took a firm grip on the future she had outlined for herself. She opened her social media accounts and started removing objectionable posts. Dear Lord there were some nasty people out there. Some thought she was a harlot, others offered to do lewd things to her…

She didn't realize she was making noises like she was being roundly beaten in a boxing ring until Vito asked sharply, "What are you reading?"

"I want to connect with a headhunter to start searching out a position for when this is over." She winced as an invitation to hook up flashed into her eyes with a photo that couldn't be deleted fast enough. "I have to clean up my news feeds first, before potential employers look them over. It's a minefield."

"*You* don't," he growled, reaching across to click off her phone. "Plumbers exist to clean up sewage. I've already assigned you a PR assistant. She'll meet with you this afternoon and scrub all of this."

The last thing she wanted was to accept more generosity from him, but she was too grateful to refuse.

"And I'll see that you have a suitable position when the time comes so don't put out feelers for a job yet. It sends the wrong message."

"What does 'suitable' mean?"

"Something equivalent or better to the position you had, so you're not set back in your career. I've discussed it with Paolo and you'll receive a glowing recommendation, a severance package and a settlement for the damage caused by our leaving you in the position of working with Jensen despite having him under investigation. We've agreed that if we had removed you when we became suspicious, the photos wouldn't have happened, so we'll be accepting responsibility for that. We'll work out the exact details once we have Jensen on the ropes."

She blinked, stunned. Inside her chest, her heart rose like the sun from behind dark mountains, beaming light through her whole being. Lightness. The weight of being mistrusted lifted and something like hope dawned in her for the first time since she'd walked into Nadine's office and seen those photos.

"You believe me?" The words were very tentative. She could barely take it in.

"I do." His expression was grave, but there was a hard light in his eyes, not hostile, but daunting. It leaned even more impact to his words as he said, "These actions against you will not go unpunished."

She didn't fear him in that moment, but she recognized that he was a man to be feared.

And she was so relieved to have him on her side, so touched that he believed her, she grew teary and had to look away, unable to even voice a heartfelt, *Thank you.*

"But for now your occupation is 'mistress.'"

She flung her head around to confront him. "Did you say that to make me angry?"

He didn't glance up from flicking the screen on his tablet. "I said it because it's true."

"Oh, well, pray tell, what are the duties of that position? Does it come with benefits?" *Shut up, Gwyn.*

He took his time letting her regret that impulsive outburst, slowly lifting his attention to scan her expression while a faint smile played around his lips.

"Amusing me is your primary function," he said, adding a sardonic, "Check."

Then he had the audacity to let his gaze take a leisurely tour down her new top. It was a simple low-necked, peach-colored silk with a pleat at her cleavage. Not particularly sexy, but he seemed to look right through it, making her breasts feel heavy and her nipples tight. She found herself pressing her jeans-clad thighs together as a throb hit where he'd caressed her in this very backseat yesterday.

"We've covered the benefits," he added. "And that you may take advantage of them as often as you see fit."

"And this is supposed to fill up my nine-to-five?" she shot back, trying to cover her pulsing response, flicking her glance at the closed privacy screen while she willed her fierce blush to recede.

"I can't make love to you *all* day, *cara*. I have responsibilities."

She tried to send him a disgusted glare, but anticipation curled through her despite herself, melting her insides and turning her on. Yes, his low voice and sexy promise made her hot, curse him.

"Did you relive it last night?" he asked in a low tone of lusty pleasure. "I did. I wanted you to come to me, so I could feel you fall apart like that again. Under me this time."

Her stomach swooped and she turned her face to the window, trying to hide that she had toyed with the idea of going to him. She had ached with desire and had had to fight against the urge.

"I need to find healthier ways to deal with my situation than cheap sexual gratification," she said.

"Stop calling it cheap." His voice lashed with quick anger, making all the hairs rise on her body.

Now who was angry and who was laughing? She looked back at him and let him see her smug delight in getting a rise out of him.

"I'm sorry," she said with mock regret. "This is becoming quite expensive for you, isn't it? Because if you won't let me get a real job, you'll have to cover the lease on my flat." It was a childish jab and promptly fell flat.

"That's already in the works."

Her smarmy grin fell away.

He smiled at having drawn the wind from her sails. "I've had mistresses before," he added calmly, sobering a few degrees as he added, "Never one who has moved in with me, but we have a message to broadcast. I've assigned you an assistant. She'll send you our calendar shortly."

Moved in? *Our* calendar?

"I thought I was going back to my flat." She glanced toward the driver who had said he had her address.

"To get your passport and any other personal items you don't want to leave for the movers. Am I speaking English? Why are you staring at me like that?"

"When did I agree to move in with you? Do I get my own room?"

"Do you want one?" he asked, sounding oh-so-reasonable against her high pitch of disbelief, but the knowing slant to his half-closed lids made the question not just annoying, but far too rhetorical.

She didn't know how to be sophisticated and blasé about agreeing to be his lover. She was still fighting the longing to. Deep down, however, she knew she wanted to go to bed with him, and very likely would, which was the most aggravating part of it all.

Thankfully her phone buzzed. She glanced to see her new assistant was loading her calendar.

Gwyn scanned through, seeing that she had legal meetings, appointments with her PR assistant, stylists, boutiques—

"A *spa*?" she said sharply to Vito.

"All the women in my family frequent it. Don't worry. It's secure."

Luncheons, dinners—

"Berlin?"

"I have meetings." He shrugged.

London, Paris, back to Milan then three stops in Asia.

"What am I doing while you're working in all these places?" she asked, mind whirling.

"You'll have a security detail. Do whatever you want. Shop, visit the museums. You won't have as much time as you think. I'll need you at my side quite often."

She spent the rest of the drive answering questions for her assistant: Did she have any special dietary requirements or allergies? Any requests for products to have on hand at Vito's apartment or while she traveled? Was she due for any dental or medical appointments that should be scheduled? What about prescription refills?

More birth control pills? Was that what she was asking, Gwyn wondered with mild hysteria?

When they arrived in the city, they went straight to her building where a handful of photographers quickly snapped to attention from slouching on scooters and hovering on stoops. Vito's security guards kept them at a respectful distance and movers arrived shortly after Gwyn entered her flat.

The place was untouched, her plate with toast crumbs from a few days ago still sitting by the sink, but everything had changed. Not just her life, but there was something in *her* that was changing. She was a self-sufficient person, didn't want to look to Vito to rescue her like some kind of damsel needing a white knight, but as he gave instructions and spoke to her landlord to assure him the crowds at the entrance to the building would cease now that she was leaving, she felt grateful to have him on her side.

She hated feeling weak and managed and powerless, but if someone else was stealing control of her life, she was glad the rudder had wound up in his unerring hands.

She trusted him, she realized. It was a weird sort of trust. He could and probably would hurt her, but he wasn't making any false promises not to. He wouldn't lie to her, even if the truth was harsh and unpalatable.

His governance over her world proved very advantageous when she made her statement to the police, too. Had she been merely a midlevel bank employee with no connections or legal team behind her, her complaint probably wouldn't have been such a priority, but she was assured charges against her masseuse would be forthcoming.

The rest of the day passed in a blur. There was a very short press conference announcing the birth of Paolo's son, Vito's assumption of his cousin's position for the next few weeks and he confirmed rumors that a formal internal investigation had been launched against an unnamed, but high profile account.

"For privacy and legal reasons, we can't expound on that," Vito said.

Then he sent a look to Gwyn that said everything his mouth did not. His expression spoke of regret and guardianship and the suppressed anger of a warrior who must wait for the war. Which might have been a bit of overacting for the cameras, but she thought it had its seeds in what he had said earlier about Jensen not going unpunished.

And she was touched all over again.

The press conference had been held at a hotel where Vito was due to meet with various heads of the bank's branches before attending a mixer with those same people, their spouses and an exclusive list of their top-tier investors.

"It was scheduled a year ago, long before any of this hit the fan," he said, sending her to a penthouse suite with an entourage who coached her on everything from staying on message—*The investigation is ongoing. I can't comment.*—to how to lengthen her lashes most effectively.

She was mentally and emotionally exhausted when they all finally left her alone, seriously wishing she could go to bed instead of having to go out.

Then Vito materialized from the second bedroom like a freshly groomed panther, his black tuxedo a second skin, the white of his pleated shirt and bow tie a blaze that set off his swarthy skin tone, hollow cheeks and straight black brows. His hair, just a shade too long to be a conservative business cut, gave him the perfect balance between decadent playboy and powerful executive.

His silk pocket square exactly matched the reflective, lake blue of her gown.

She'd never worn anything so elegant or daring, with its strapless bodice and low back. The sweep of the skirt was gathered in loose edges, forming a slit over her left leg, and was ruched together with a sparkling broach on her hip, making her feel graceful and sexy at once.

She felt sensual. Beautiful. And, as she stood looking at the beautiful man before her, she felt for the first time like she was his match.

Vito was trying to make it to the end of a trying day. He understood the concerns of those around him, the questioning of his choice in female companionship, but he couldn't understand why he was so angered by all of it. He kept telling himself it was the bank he wanted to defend. To protect.

But it was Gwyn. He wanted to sweep a sword

through the air to cut down all this resistance against his being with her.

And this was why.

She stood before him like a water deity, wearing that swirl of river blue and sapphires that gleamed like bubbles against her neck and ears. Her hair was caught in a low knot against the back of her neck, wisps framing her introspective expression, mysterious and enthralling.

She was a prize, a weapon, an illicit substance. She was something he wanted. Badly.

His libido was becoming a monster, first hooked by spending nearly every moment with her for the past forty-eight hours, then feeling her absence as he'd pushed her to the sidelines to weather attacks from close quarters.

It had left him keyed up, mood balanced on a knife's edge, the outlaw in him looking to ignore any sort of rules or propriety and simply take her, make her his. This wasn't the first time he'd chafed against the constraints he placed upon himself, but he always maintained this veneer of civility painted onto him by the family who had kept him alive, safe and living within the law.

She didn't want cheap gratification, he reminded himself, and heard Paolo again. *If she's a victim, don't make her more of one.* He kept remembering that look in her eye as they'd played house for an hour with Paolo's children. If only the world understood how laughable it was to think *she* was inferior to *him*.

"You look nice," he said gruffly, trying not to let the vision she made break the shackles controlling him. He moved to hold the door. "Let's get this over with."

She made a noise that might have been one of injury and muttered, "That's what she said," as she passed him into the hall.

"*What* did you just say?" he asked tightly.

Gwyn grappled her feelings back into their box, telling herself to quit taking his lack of real interest in her as a slight.

"It's just something people say. One of those online memes," she said, striding purposefully beside him toward the elevator. "Why are you so grouchy?"

The hotel was pure opulence, the carpets cushioning each step, the rail dripping leafy plants in terraced layers down to the lobby forty stories below.

He pressed the call button for the elevator and said, "I'm not."

She glanced around, saw they were alone and said, "You know, we may not have much, but I thought we had honesty. If you don't want to tell me, say it's none of my business. But don't lie."

His gaze widened at her audacity, making her swallow. But honestly. She was doing everything she was told, letting him treat her like a puppet after she'd already been misused. What else did he want from her?

The elevator arrived and an older couple stepped off, leaving them to enter the empty car alone, replacing what might have been an air of relaxed camaraderie with a charged energy that bounced off the refined walls.

At least it wasn't one of those glass boxes that made you feel airsick as you descended. It was red velvet and had mirrored panels split by a flat rectangle of gold for a handrail. A chipper, understated soft shoe drifted from the speakers, sounding incongruous.

"If you must have the truth, *cara*, I've been warned several times today that our relationship is ill-advised," he said, stabbing at a floor number, then thumbing hard into the door close button. "I know they're right, but I don't care. I want you, anyway. If we'd stayed in the room, I would have kept you there."

"Really?" she derided. "I thought I just asked you not to lie to me? Because you've never once acted like you wanted anything to do with me."

"Ha!" He punched the side of his fist into the red emergency button, stalling the elevator with a jar and a short buzz, making her stagger and reach for the rail. "The very fact that you can't read the signs tells me how ill-suited you are for an affair. But, just so we're crystal clear, *cara*, I don't care about that, either. *I want you.*"

She couldn't look away from him, fascinated by the way his gold-brown eyes shot glittering shards of bronze.

He stepped closer, setting one hand then the other on the wall next to her head, leaning in. "I wanted you when you smiled across the lobby and you were already under suspicion, so I couldn't do a damn thing about it. I wanted you when I looked at this…" His boiling metal gaze slid down her front, scalding her. "And I knew every other man in the world was looking at you, too." His gaze flashed up, bright and piercing. "I want to kill each and every one of them," he added tightly. "Especially Jensen."

Her knuckle bumped his side and she realized her hand had lifted of its own volition, moving to press against her chest and keep her heart inside its cage. It slammed hard and fast.

He looked at her splayed fingers. "Scared?"

"I honestly didn't think you…" Her voice trailed off as his expression hardened with accusation.

"How could you not know? You look at me constantly. I *feel* it. How could you not be aware that I'm watching you, too?" He picked up her hand and pressed it to his own chest, where his heart punched against her palm. "You felt this in the car, when just my touch made you scream with pleasure. How could you not know it's the same for me?"

Emotion pressed at the backs of her eyes and thickened her throat.

He watched her struggle to swallow and cupped his hand under her jaw, palm against her throbbing artery, thumb caressing the hollow below her ear.

"The only thing holding me back, *mia bella*, is

your indecision. Have you made up your mind yet? Do you want cheap, physical gratification?" The bitterness in his tone scraped at something in her, making her squirm in a kind of guilt.

She had hurt him with that? She searched his eyes, the windows into his soul. "What else would it be?" she asked in a near whisper.

His lips hardened and his brow lowered in consternation. "I don't know. But it would be a hell of a lot more than that."

She lifted her hand to the side of his face, drew him in and pressed a kiss of apology onto his mouth. It was perfect and sweet and healing.

And a mistake.

With a moan from her and a tortured groan from him, they laced themselves together, mouths opening with instant passion, dragged together like magnets meeting its attractor. His fingers dug into her back, her bottom, crushing her close. She arched into his steely body, loving his strength and the smell of him and that firm evidence of arousal that was not purely incidental, but his reaction to *her*.

He pressed her into the wall with his body, stilling the rock of her hips with a hard pin of his own. "You want me," he said against her lips. It was a demand for confirmation.

"I do," she admitted with an ache of helpless need.

"Now?"

"Wh-what?" She opened her eyes to see a fiery passion in him that was barely controlled. This man who seemed to have command of the entire world was so affected by her, he was looking at her with a kind of desperation. She thought she could feel each pulse pound in him, rocking his entire being.

"Here?" she asked. She was achy and heavy and ready. The thought of waiting until they were upstairs—it was too far.

This was insanity. Complete insanity.

"No?" He shuffled closer, feet between hers, one hand going to the slit in her skirt, finding her bare thigh and stroking across her skin like magic. "If not here, say so now."

She might have hung on to a shred of decorum if he hadn't found the front of her lace undies and traced lightly while his mouth found the side of her neck at the same time. Need flooded through her at that light caress. She gasped with longing, clinging to his shoulders, trying to keep her knees locked so she wouldn't wilt right to the floor.

"Open my pants," he said, breath hot on her skin while the nibble of his lips made her shiver with pleasure and that exploring touch worked past the edge of lace into wetness and need. She made a guttural sound of pure excitement as he circled and pressed the swollen bud he found. His other hand was gathering her skirt out of the way, lifting her bare thigh to his hip, opening her to his flagrant touch.

"We can't," she gasped, but her hands worked the button on his pants, the fly. She had never tunneled her hand into the heated front of a man's trousers, but there was his shape filling her palm, naked and hot and silky. He was commando, shockingly bare to her touch, smooth with a graze of rough hair at the base, so steely and thickly aroused she gasped and clenched in anticipation.

He bent his knees, urging her to line him up as he shifted her underwear to the side. He traced his thick tip along her seam, parted, sliding easily against her then probing. "Do I need a condom?"

Late for that, wasn't it? She was dying! Panting with excitement.

"I'm on the pill," she managed to say, moving in invitation. She wanted him so badly. *Now.*

Their breaths mingled. His nostrils flared as he found her opening and pressed with more purpose. Nerves made her stiffen slightly, but she was eager, anxious as she looked into his eyes, wanting him to like it, wanting this to be good.

"Oh," she whispered as he pushed the tip in, stretching her. Her gaze clouded and her breaths grew uneven. When she clenched on him, little shock waves of pleasure jolted through her. Her eyelids grew heavy and wanted to close.

He pressed farther in, his weight driving her against something that dug into her back. She wriggled, making a noise of discomfort. "The rail—"

He smoothly lifted her, one hand going under her bottom where he balanced her above that infernal rail and then he was firmly seated all the way in, eye to eye with her. It was incredibly intimate. Man and woman. Steel and silk. Their panting breaths humid against each other's lips.

"Hold on to me," he rasped.

She closed her legs around his waist, twined her arms over his shoulders.

He moved, watching her expression as he withdrew and returned, driving in deep, holding there a moment, then dragging out slow, tantalizing her to new heights, arousing her with each thrust. Then he built the tempo to swift thrusts that were exciting and delicious and sent her racing up the slopes of need.

She clung to him with every part of her. He was hard everywhere, tense and determined. Her lips ached to be kissed, but she needed air. She couldn't look away from his gaze, watchful, waiting, demanding. It was too wild, too erotic, too scorchingly fast. She was there, right there, shuddering and flying apart. Finally closing her eyes as the pleasure detonated into something otherworldly.

A deeply animalistic noise left him as he arched deep and pulsed inside her, holding her in that state of ecstasy.

She gloried in the moment, body electrified as they completely possessed each other, united in this moment of culmination.

CHAPTER EIGHT

GWYN COULDN'T BELIEVE she had let him do that to her. Her legs were still trembling as she joined him inside the ballroom, having slipped into the ladies' room the minute they left the elevator to recover herself.

"*Cara*, please meet some friends of mine," he said, settling his arm around her as he introduced her.

It was different. She was different and they were different. Her world had been upended all over again. The sexual awareness was still there, but instead of being a sharp, unmet need, it was a deep, perilous knowledge. She knew what her body was capable of. He did. They both knew what he could do to her, how he could strip her of willpower and blind her with desire. She wondered if she had really done the same to him because he didn't seem as affected.

His arm sat heavier on her, more possessive, but when his glance came into her eyes, his held the light of memory and male satisfaction, but none of her wariness.

She was suffering all the same crush and attraction and fascination, but it was even more painful now. Before, she had yearned for him to match this feeling. Now she knew it didn't matter if he did. She was lost regardless.

It made the stares and the curled lips and the dismissive way people treated her as he introduced her all the harder to bear.

She said nothing, still wondering how on earth she would survive Vito let alone the rest of all that had happened. It made her desperate for reassurance, but he was no help, standing here looking indifferent, letting one of his executives from New York talk his ear off about some policy Vito had assigned him to write.

To her, it sounded a lot like a guy trying to impress the boss by telling him how hard he was working, rather than actually doing the work.

Meanwhile, Gwyn realized she knew the woman from the Charleston branch who had just caught her eye. Here would come a gauntlet of questions. This was going to be the worst night of her life.

The moment she tried to excuse herself, however, Vito's arm hardened on her.

"I should say hello to Ms. Tamsin," Gwyn said, caught between homesickness and dread. She would love to hear the news on her former colleagues, but really didn't want to talk about herself.

"I'll come with you." Vito nodded at the man who'd been pontificating.

"But I want your advice!" the executive blurted.

Gwyn was so far into her own head, she completely misplaced where she was and who they were talking to. In that moment, a coworker was asking for guidance so she offered it. “Why don’t you use the UK model as a template? Tailor it to US regulations and plug in that bit about interstate transfers. The section on overseas rates should work almost word for word.”

The surprised pause and dumbfounded stares from both men were almost laughable, except Gwyn realized how badly she’d overstepped and instantly wanted to die of embarrassment. She never would have spoken to Oscar Fabrizio or any other higher-up that way. No, she would have done that work for him, she thought privately, and let him take the credit. Such was the life of lower-level administrators.

The executive was taken aback and glanced between her and Vito, as if to say, *Are you going to let your porn star girlfriend talk to me like that?*

“Excellent suggestion,” Vito said. “Why reinvent the wheel? I’ll expect to see the draft tomorrow,” he told his executive and walked her away.

“I’m sorry,” she mumbled.

“For what?”

“Interjecting like that.”

“Why? You were right. I would have thought of it myself eventually, but I wasn’t really listening. Too busy thinking of something else,” he said with a pointed look that shot sexual heat from her heart to her loins. "I've never gone without a condom before. That was exciting. *Grazie, mia bella.*"

Her hand tightened on his sleeve as her knees wobbled, making him smile like a shark.

The rest of the evening was a trial, but she got through it. And when they were leaving, he surprised her by taking her downstairs to a waiting car instead of back up to the penthouse he'd already paid for.

"What about the early morning meetings you have here tomorrow?" She tilted her head at the hotel. "I thought that's why we were staying here."

"I want you in my bed."

Her skin tightened in reaction. "Okay."

Vittorio was not a weak or needy man. He loved his family and would certainly be a lesser man without them, but he considered himself a supporter of *them*, not the other way around. He wasn't a dependent personality, either. He drank a glass of wine most days because it was a cultural habit, not because he was addicted.

Gwyn was another story.

As he tied his tie, he glanced at her sleeping form reflected beyond his shoulder, brunette hair spilled across his pillow where she'd rolled to hug it when he'd risen, murmuring a sleepy and satisfied, "Thank you," before falling back asleep.

Words she had promised him he would never hear, he thought edgily, still high on the powerful orgasm they'd shared from a very lazy missionary lock in the predawn hour, the paroxysm holding them gasping for long, exquisite moments.

It had been two weeks and, if anything, the chemistry between them was stronger. If he was in her presence, he wanted to touch her. If he touched her, he wanted to have sex with her.

His desire was becoming the sort of all-consuming hunger that he arranged the rest of his life around. If he had other thoughts, they tended to be of the reckoning kind: dark acts of retaliation against Jensen and his cohorts. He wanted justice for Gwyn, but not necessarily the legal kind that would put an end to their reason for being together.

"I'm jealous," Gwyn said in a soft morning voice that lifted the hairs all over his body.

"Of whom?" he asked, reaching for his suit jacket, shrugging it on like armor.

He'd had these sorts of conversations before, but he had to admit to shock that Gwyn would have any reason to feel possessive. Had he even looked at another woman since meeting her? If he had, it was a comparison that Gwyn always won. Not just in looks, either. If he heard a woman laugh, he thought the sound too sharp or coarse, not the perfect joyful huskiness of Gwyn's. None seemed to have her same intuitive ability with conversation either, steering seamlessly from business to small talk to current events. His lack of interest in other women might have worried him if his libido hadn't been showing such vigor and health in bed with this one.

"You," she answered ruefully, rolling onto her back and throwing her arm over her head. "Going to work." She touched the headboard, looking up to the pattern her finger found and traced.

Her remark didn't entirely surprise him. He might have had innumerable mistresses who expected to be supported, but his sisters and the bank's abundance of female employees told him that many women enjoyed their careers as much as men did. Gwyn was bright and confident and had had clear goals before Jensen had derailed her. A life of leisure was not something she had aspired to—which was yet another side of her character that set her apart and shone a favorable light upon her in his eyes.

It was also why he enjoyed supporting her. She didn't expect to be spoiled so her reaction was priceless when he collared her with precious stones and shackled her with gold bracelets. Her protests against his generosity were refreshing, her newness to belonging to a man endearing.

He moved to the bed and lowered to hitch his hip beside hers, splaying his hand over the rumpled sheet that covered her belly. "I thought you enjoyed the art exhibit yesterday?" He had liked watching her face light with enthusiasm as she had told him about it last night.

"I did. I'm not sure your bodyguards did, though." She covered his hand, traced her light touch over the backs of his fingers, sending a ripple of pleasure down his back, as if he was a wolf being petted by a maiden.

"Well-secured places like art galleries make their job easy. They're happy to follow you around one." That wasn't the real issue, he could tell, but he didn't know what else she needed to hear. Perhaps, "Rather than go back to Milan when I finish here, why don't we take a few days on the water?" he suggested. "I'll hire a yacht."

Her gaze met his. "I feel like I'm back in my childhood, moving around before I can establish myself, not even trying to make friends because there's no point."

He frowned, having supposed that she connected with her friends online when he wasn't around, but she never mentioned any conversations or told anecdotes, he realized. She'd already told him that the family she did have was a very loose tie. She was still too embarrassed to speak directly to her stepfather and was keeping to short texts with her stepbrother.

He couldn't imagine living in that sort of social desert. He had curtailed a lot of his nonbusiness dinners because of work pressures and was sidestepping family occasions to avoid awkward questions about his relationship with Gwyn, but he was Italian. An active social life was in his biological makeup.

"Why did you move so often?" he asked her.

She shrugged. "Every reason. Lost job, better job, good luck, bad luck, harassment, location… I think the biggest reason was that Mom had itchy feet. That's why she married my dad, to move to America. She and Henry were going to travel once I finished school." Her fingertips smoothed under his cuff, tracing the band of his watch. "I wanted to see the world, too, but by moving to a new city and settling in, so I could absorb the culture and become part of the community."

Whatever friendships she'd made in Milan had been blown apart by the photos and her termination. He hadn't forbidden her from contacting any of her coworkers or neighbors, but she had isolated herself and he'd been pleased to keep things simple. He wondered now if he should make more of an effort to draw her into his own circles, but to what end? This was a temporary affair, not a relationship.

And knowing their time together was finite, he found himself very unwilling to share her.

"No news from Paolo about how much longer the investigation will take?" she asked.

"No," he said so abruptly her eyes widened and a shadow of injury crept across the back of her gaze. He mentally kicked himself for revealing the brute that he was, but her question almost sounded as though she was anxious to end things and he wasn't ready.

"Living in limbo is hard," she said in stiff explanation, trying to sit up.

He gathered her tense form into his lap, looking at

the pugnacious glare she tilted up at him. He pressed a kiss against her firmly closed mouth.

"I'm hearing you," he told her, thinking about those times when he caught a faraway, melancholy expression on her face. He had put those moments down to her distress over the photos, but there was more to it, he realized now. She was a woman longing to put down roots. "I'm not dismissing you. But there's nothing I can do right now."

"And nothing I can do either, apparently."

"Fold my socks?" he suggested, since she often nagged him to pick his up.

She snapped her teeth at him in playful retaliation.

He kissed her again and this time she softened and kissed him back.

But he was still thinking about her discontent when he broke from his meeting with the Hong Kong consortium and picked up a message from Paolo: *Fabrizio is asking for leniency in exchange for full disclosure. We could see charges against Jensen early next week.*

The tide was turning.

The need for their affair was almost over.

Gwyn was in a type of shock as they returned to Vito's penthouse less than a week later, mind still caught up in all that had just been said at the press conference and after it. *Be careful what you wish for*, she thought bleakly. She had been anxious to embark on her future and here it was.

"I wish to say a special thank-you to Miss Ellis for her patience and unwavering integrity during this entire process," Paolo had said. "Due to the sensitive nature of the investigation, we asked her not to make any public comments during a time that has obviously been very distressing for her."

The cameras' lenses had shifted to where she had stood next to Vito, trying to capture her reaction, which she had fought to keep noncommittal. Inside, she'd been screaming in agony and still was. This was it. *The End.*

Paolo's private words to her afterward were what had really done her in. Handlers had moved them into an anteroom and scattered. Vito had stepped away to call his assistant with some instructions.

"Grazie," Paolo had said to Gwyn, not showing any reaction when he shook her hand and found it clammy. "We will pursue defamation charges on your behalf and that could result in prison time for Jensen, but I realize that does nothing to compensate you for all you've lost. Vito promised you a settlement, *sì*? Hire a good lawyer and begin those negotiations immediately. I want a number so I can add it to our list of damages when Jensen is tried."

"Of course," Gwyn had murmured, as if she had the first idea how to hire any kind of lawyer, let alone a "good" one. Her mind had started buzzing the minute Vito had called her to say he was sending a car and was bursting with a bigger swarm of bees over how abruptly this press conference ended the need for their affair.

She was devastated. Her very nascent and juvenile crush had become something real and deep and heart-wrenching.

She had started to think of his beautiful apartment as her home.

Vittorio had modern tastes and liked space around him. The penthouse had high white ceilings and three bedrooms, one that he used as an office, off a tiled upper hallway that he called a loft. It was nothing so modest as that. It was a second story. The main bathroom had His and Hers powder rooms on opposite ends of a tub that they easily, and frequently, shared. This flat was wall-to-wall understated luxury, from the designer furniture to the kitchen that sparkled with stainless steel functionality, positioned to allow the cook to visit with guests while stirring and chopping.

High-end art, lush plants and family photos rounded off the space into a haven of warmth and welcome. Her snapshot of her almost family, her own image with her arms around Henry and her mother, sat on the night table next to her side of the bed.

Gwyn swallowed, trying to hide her devastation at leaving all of this, along with the man who lived here, by kicking off her heels beside the front closet, then realized she would have to pack them. She couldn't wrap her brain around what that would entail so she moved to where she'd left her tablet on the sectional before the big screen TV, pretending she was checking email.

"Are you hungry?" Vito asked behind her, shrugging out of his suit jacket and tossing it across the back of the sofa. "I'm going to make coffee."

She wasn't, but she loved cooking with him, enjoying the foreplay of brushing bodies, senses stimulated by the aroma of fresh ingredients, the sizzle of a pan and the rich textures and flavors they seemed to create together.

The full scope of all that she was losing gripped her and she lifted her head to stare blindly through the bright windows.

"Cara?" He was right behind her, making her start. "What's wrong?"

"Nothing." *Everything.*

His gaze dropped to her tablet. "Something has upset you? Do not tell me you're reading reactions to today's press conference. Stop polluting your head that way."

"No, um—" She glanced at the tablet, saw Travis's latest message, started to gloss past it, then decided to confront it. Just pull the bandage off in one ruthless yank. She showed him what Travis had written.

I saw the press conference. Does this mean you're coming home?

Vito's gaze came up and slammed into hers. He was so handsome. Brutally, impossibly handsome with his white shirt and striped tie and tailored pants with their knifelike creases, then black leather shoes glossed to a mirror finish. She didn't know any other man who could wear a vest with the buttons offset at an angle like that, the edge piped in silver, and look so suave.

She longed to trace that piping, touch those buttons. She very much needed the connection that seemed to have been building between them with each physical encounter, but what did they really have? Sex. That was all.

"We haven't really talked about the next steps. I imagine I will be leaving?" she said, insides hollow. "Now that we don't have to pretend anymore?"

They weren't pretending. That's what his cocked brow said.

She licked her lips. "Because it would make it pretty obvious we got together just for show if I left right away, wouldn't it?" Tossing the tablet onto the sofa, she jerked a shoulder. "I could say I'm going to see family and we could let it die off from there."

"We could," he said carefully, so emotionless a scalding pain rose behind her breastbone.

For a moment she couldn't even breathe, let alone speak or move. Then she found a smile of false bravado and brought her hands to the sides of his head.

His hot palms settled on her hips, holding her off as he gave her a questioning look.

She didn't have a very strong grip on her emotions, and keeping anything from him these days was pretty much impossible, but she tried to affect nonchalance.

"Don't worry. I'm not staking a claim. I'll figure

it out in a little while. But I'd like to leave you with something to remember."

Then, because she had spent a great deal of time devoting herself to learning what turned him on, she did everything she could to arouse him. She rarely instigated lovemaking unless they were in bed. It was shyness and lack of confidence, but today she left inhibition at the door and pressed herself against him suggestively.

She ran her hands over him with the proprietary touch she usually suppressed. His shoulders were a landscape of masculinity, appealing to the primal woman in her that sought protection and provision. His buttons opened to, first, the warm silk of his shirt, then the satin of his skin, with the fine hairs on his breastbone and a dark arrow to his navel that teased her lips as she kissed what she exposed. His nipples were sharp against her tongue and her teasing made him suck in a quick breath.

She kissed him, not just letting him know she was receptive, but taking the initiative, not hinting that she wanted to make love, but demanding it. It was exhilarating to be this assertive.

He let her bare his chest and open his pants, swiveling so he leaned his hips against the back of the sofa and stepped his feet apart, drawing her into the space. Then he cupped her face so he could kiss her, not taking control, but not passive. Never passive.

Her own clothes loosened, suit jacket falling away,

bow at her neck tugging then falling into ribbons of blue polka dots on white. Vito drew back long enough to pull the sheer confection over her head then brought her against him again, skin to skin, both of them murmuring approving noises.

Vito had experienced the advances of women in the past. Often it was a power play or a quid pro quo of some kind. Sometimes he relaxed and enjoyed it, other times he set the pace that suited him.

Gwyn, guileless, sensual Gwyn, undid him. She was so very entrancing in her conservative exterior and her abandonment to lovemaking, especially today as she licked into his mouth, rubbing against him in a way that was not so much practiced as pure. She was trying to turn him on, but the way she grew bright-eyed and flushed with hectic color was even more arousing.

When she released his belt and opened his pants, he let her drag them down his thighs, watching her drop to her knees and loving the sight of her taking him in hand. The sensations of her wet worship, the encompassing heat and delicate suction, had him tempted to let her take him all the way. This *was* something he would remember for the rest of his life. He would never forget her. He had known that before she'd begun anointing him this way.

But if they were saying goodbye, he wanted to do the same to her. To make this last. To create the sort of memory that would sustain them both for the rest of their lives.

That knowledge was a sharp twist in his gut that allowed him to pull her to her feet, turning her so she faced the back of the sofa.

"Wait. I want—"

"Are you not doing what I want, *mia bella*?" He paused in bringing her skirt up, waiting. "Giving me something to remember you by?"

Her knuckles were white where she gripped the leather. "Yes," she whispered. "But I want to see you. Kiss you."

"You will," he promised her, kissing her bare shoulder, then drawing back to memorize the sight of plum wool bunched on the small of her back as he pressed her to bend forward. He stroked his hand over pale white cheeks wearing a line of amethyst lace. Those he dispatched to around her ankles in a moment, caressing her where she was plump and wet, hearing her whimper under his touch, back arching, shoulders shuddering with pleasure.

"We will always have this," he vowed, pressing into her. "Now come for me." He shifted his hand so he was giving her all the pleasure she could bear. "Surrender to me. It's what I love the most," he told her, opening his mouth on her nape, losing himself to the delight of thrusting into her, barely holding on as she suddenly gasped and clenched in strong pulses around him. Her gorgeous cries of fulfillment went through him like church bells.

He petted her as he carefully withdrew and

kicked out of his pants. Then he scooped up her still-quivering body and carried her toward the stairs.

"You didn't—"

"I know exactly what I have and haven't done, *mia bella.*" His ears were ringing with the pulse hammering upward from the damp, urgent flesh between his thighs. "If you think I'm going to let our last time be a one-sided dalliance in the front room, you haven't learned one damned thing about me or what I expect from my mistress."

It wasn't unusual for them to make love two or three times in a day. Sometimes it was a rush of passion, sometimes a slow, sultry buildup.

It had never been quite such a complete immersion. They ignored the phone when it rang, ignored the growl of their stomachs, barely even spoke except to encourage or compliment or groan incomprehensibly.

Finally, when it was well and truly dark beyond the windows, they landed weak and sated and aching with sensual exhaustion, limbs tangled, quiet and still at last.

The sense of closeness between them was so acute that Gwyn could barely comprehend that it was over, but it was. Those panting moments when their hearts had beat in unison had merely been physical compatibility. Nothing more.

Shifting her arm off her stinging eyes, she decided

a trip to the ladies room might be in order to keep herself from revealing how hard this was for her.

"Stay," he said as she began to rise.

A helpless noise escaped her. "Honestly, Vito, I don't think I can. That was…a lot." Her loins were stinging and tender, her muscles quivering with overuse.

A gruff noise escaped him, part humor, part apology. He came up on an elbow and scooped her beneath him, heavy on her as he pinned her to the mattress. "That's quite a compliment if you think I have anything left in me," he growled, nose going into her neck and inhaling. "I mean stay in Milan. This doesn't have to end here and now."

She stilled. "You're asking me to stay as your mistress?"

"Sì."

The room was dark shadows and rumpled blankets; her world narrowed to the warmth of his lips against her collarbone. He didn't see her wince of agony at the term. He might sometimes refer to her as his lover, but that was a euphemism for what she really was. She knew that and she had justified what she was letting herself become as necessary for their ruse.

But that was no longer necessary.

"Because it would look better for the press?" she asked.

"Because we're good together."

That surprised her, making her heart leap as

though he'd admitted to deep, abiding affection even though she knew he only meant they knocked each other off the bed with the intensity of physical pleasure they gave each other.

If she stayed with him, wouldn't that allow time for him to develop deeper feelings toward her, though? It was the kind of treacherous, self-delusion all women were capable of, when they were half in love with a man who didn't love them back. She knew it, but she was still tempted to let him talk her into staying. To see.

She traced the line of his spine and lightly searched for proof that he might already be harboring feelings toward her.

"What if I don't want to?" she asked.

His turn to go completely still. He lifted his head and in the muted light she saw his hard mouth twist. "I'm not a man who begs, *cara.* Be careful about bluffing. I'll call you on it."

She ought to be happy he'd gone so far as to tell her he wanted her to stay, she supposed. It *was* quite an admission from such a self-sufficient man. One who could have his choice among women.

"It's not an ultimatum," she said, trying to hide her hurt behind a neutral tone. "I told you when we first met that I don't have affairs. Relying on you goes against everything I've tried to become. I ought to start salvaging my life, not leave it on hold."

His tense hand on her waist grew heavy. "I respect your independence. I do," he assured her. "But your life is already on hold, I carry some of the fault for that and I have the means to support you while you give real thought to your next steps. Let me do this for you, *cara*."

I respect you. Such a small phrase and it moved her so very deeply to hear it. How could she not stay and try to nurture that into something even more meaningful?

"I don't want to lose that respect," she said, hearing his breath catch and taking heart from it. It almost sounded like he was bracing himself. "But I do enjoy the sex."

If the noise he made sounded to her like relief, she knew that was wishful thinking. He was amused, which had been her goal. Keep it light. Don't let him know how emotionally dependent she really was.

"And I'm going to have to insist on more frequent feedings," she added, trying to rise. "I suppose I have to cook again?"

"Two words, *cara*," he growled, flattening her on her back and setting his teeth against her shoulder. "Bite me."

CHAPTER NINE

"Good job on the lawyer," Paolo said dryly as he opened the door to his home to them a few nights later.

Gwyn was a bundle of nerves, not quite believing this was a mere social dinner, but Vito assured her it was. All she had done was ask casually how Lauren and the baby were getting on. Vito had called to ask and it had turned into a dinner invitation. Now, here they were.

"She's really nice, isn't she?" she said to Paolo, barely tracking the conversation as the old-world beauty of the house dazzled her. Vito had told her as they drove in that the house had been in the family for generations. It was set on a property that had to be worth millions of euros given its size and location. What charmed her more was the way the high ceilings and Renaissance architecture and formal furniture was peppered with colorful children's toys, a baby swing and the sleek lines of a laptop on an antique escritoire.

"Nice," Paolo repeated under his breath, saying to Vito, "Did you have anything to do with her choice?"

"I've stayed out of it. Why? Are we likely to lose these?" Vito plucked at his shirt.

"My stepbrother found her for me," Gwyn hurried to say. "I didn't know who else to ask. Why? Is she awful?"

"Depends which side of the table you're on," Paolo said smoothly. "You're on the side where she is very nice. But she's already setting a high bar for our own legal team. It will be a good exercise for them in staying sharp."

Lauren came down the stairs at that point, newborn in her arm.

After a greeting of kisses all around, she brought them through the house to the back to greet the children who were playing outside under the eye of the nanny.

"Ignore the boxes," Lauren said as they came back in, waving at the dozens piled near the back stairs. "One of the aunts has embarked on a family history book. Paolo and I have been digging relics out of attics and pantries that haven't been opened in years. It's fascinating! So many old photos and diaries. *Love* letters."

Gwyn had just taken the baby from Lauren, gathering his warm body close and glancing at Vito like she was the first person to ever cuddle a baby. It was a vulnerable moment of wanting to share her excitement and joy, maybe see what he thought of the sight of her with an infant against her heart, but he wasn't looking at her.

He and Paolo had a lightning exchange that consisted of one look of inquiry and another of an infinitesimal shake of Paolo's head replying, *No.*

If Vito realized she had seen what had just transpired, he betrayed nothing. In fact, his direct gaze, so forceful as he met hers, was a silent declaration that he had nothing to hide.

But she'd seen something. She knew it.

"That's what brought me to Italy, you know," Lauren said, moving through to the lounge where she gathered toys. "Looking up family. My grandmother had a *scandalous* affair with a married man and went home pregnant."

"Here I thought you came to Italy for me," Paolo said, holding up a red plastic bin so Lauren could drop her collection of stuffed toys and books into it.

"You're why I stayed, *mio bello,*" she said, offering her lips for a kiss.

The rest of the evening passed in entertaining conversation, excellent food and an invitation from the children to read bedtime stories. It was sweet, yet poignant, making Gwyn recall the way Vito had told her this would never be her life.

Later, as they were readying for bed, she asked him, "Did you ever live in that house?" She was still thinking about that odd moment when Lauren had mentioned love letters. Had he left some evidence of a lost crush?

"I stayed with Paolo's family at different times as a child, wherever they happened to be living. Both of our families traveled a lot, but my sisters and I were well matched in ages to Paolo and his sisters. We often had summer vacations together, that kind of thing. They were our favorite cousins and my uncle…" Vito shrugged. "I looked to him as much of a father figure as my own," he said with a hint of private irony.

"That must have been so idyllic," she said wistfully. "Did you and Paolo play with the girls? Or were you horrible sexists?"

"A little of both," he said dryly, unbuttoning his shirt. "We were never going to play with dolls without lighting their hair on fire, but if the girls wanted to play tag or hide-and-seek, we were up for it."

"And once you discovered real girls, the ones you weren't related to, I'm guessing you were never seen again?"

He didn't say anything, only left his shirt on a chair and bent to peel off his socks, leaving them on the floor. Where did he think those went? She always wound up putting them in the hamper because the housekeeper only came in every other day.

"You're not going to admit to having girlfriends back then?" she asked, brushing out her hair.

"I'm wondering why you need confirmation."

"Okay, I'll just admit that I saw you and Paolo have a silent conversation when Lauren mentioned finding letters. I wondered if you had some kind of scandalous affair in *your* past."

"I've always left it to Paolo to create the publicity stirs, keeping my own behavior to run-of-the-mill, pedestrian affairs that aren't very interesting." He held her gaze as he pulled his belt loose. "Current one being the exception."

She set her jaw, arms crossing. "Am I being too nosy? You're starting to sound hostile."

"Just bored, *cara*."

She set down her brush and worked her silver bangles over her hand, trying to hide how deeply his comment stung.

"Well, it's interesting to me," she said stiffly. "I can't imagine what a project that book will be for your aunt, having so much family history to sift through, so many people of note. I'm envious, if you want the truth. My tree is two people and I could write a single paragraph about each of them. Excuse me for being curious about yours when it has such depth."

She turned to set the bangles on the night stand and pulled off her earrings.

"A clean slate can be a good thing, *cara*. There are some family secrets better left out of the history books."

She shot him a look over her shoulder. "If that's supposed to make me less curious, you're going in the wrong direction."

"You told me you didn't want me to lie to you.

Do you remember that?" He came up behind her and found the zip at the back of her cocktail dress. "It was the day we became lovers, in the elevator."

Her dress loosened and all of her tingled with memory and fresh anticipation. How did he do that? Steal the air from her body without really touching her, just opening her dress?

"I remember," she told him, standing very still, closing her eyes because he aroused her just by standing near enough to feel his own arousal emanating off his big body.

"You said if I didn't want to talk about something I should simply say so. I don't want to talk about this, *cara*."

"Okay," she whispered, transfixed by the way her bra tightened, then loosened as he released the clasp.

"I want to suck your nipples, then I want your heels in my back as I lick my way down and make you scream my name."

She swallowed. "Okay."

Vito watched Gwyn charm the head of their legal department. She was praising the man's country after their recent visit to Zurich, where Vito had stolen a day with her for scenic driving, a hike and a picnic, opera in the evening and a late-night dinner of fondue.

It had been a day like, well, he should just admit it—it had been like a honeymoon. She had basked under his attention and he had exalted in hers. He'd never had a woman in his life who was so compatible to him, not just in bed, but out of it. Laughing or silent, naked or clothed, he always felt comfortable around her. He was always proud to have her at his side, loved showing her off.

And was half jealous of that heavyset, middle-aged counselor now, as she poured all her charm and attention in that direction, her flushed pleasure utterly captivating.

At least he could take credit for that allure of hers. Not because he'd paid for the classic suit that was tailored to make the most of her million-dollar figure, or because the smooth chignon and subdued lip color and artistic platinum pendant and earrings were also billed to him. No, he liked to think he was responsible for giving her a place where she could blossom, not just privately in his bed, where she was developing an erotic command with regard to telling him what she liked and wanted, but in public arenas.

Gwyn wasn't a bold person by nature and her photo exposé had left her self-confidence seriously dented. Vito had reminded her again and again that she had no reason to feel shame or think she owed anyone explanations. Under his tutelage, she'd regained her confidence and an attitude of self-possession that was even more hypnotic than her exquisite outer shell. He adored seeing her personality shine through like this.

"She's staying after this?" Paolo asked in an undertone, tucking away his phone.

"You disapprove?" Vito challenged lightly, but with very little actual lightness.

"I don't pass judgments on the private lives of family. You know that," Paolo said with a sardonic twist of his mouth. "If I saw impact to the bank I would comment, but I wouldn't have to, would I?"

No, he wouldn't, but Vito still wound up feeling defensive. He wasn't sure it would matter to him if this affair impacted the bank. He suspected he would carry on with Gwyn regardless.

He had intended to end things after the announcement of charges against Jensen. It would have been a tidy break without loose ends or deeply hurt feelings. Gwyn had been as prepared for it as he had. Even as she had suggested pretending a visit home to see family, he'd been thinking along the same lines.

Then she had touched him, kissed him, somehow stepped inside the shields he wore so easily against the rest of the world and imprinted herself on his very psyche. He had sought satiation that afternoon, certain that when his libido was exhausted, he'd be ready to release her.

But she'd only had to shift away from him in the bed and his entire being had been racked with agony. The single command for her to stay had slipped past his renowned self-discipline, left his lips and landed on her naked skin.

And he didn't regret it. Even though he knew she was falling in love with him. All the signs were there. She wanted to know about his childhood, wanted him to *share.* Aside from dining with Paolo and Lauren, he'd drawn a fine line between her and his personal life, but her yearning to feel connected to the broader landscape of his world, to make her place within it, was obvious.

He couldn't offer her the life she dreamed of when she held his cousin's son and scrambled his eggs in the morning and met him at the door with a kiss when he came home, though.

And cheating her of those things made him reprehensible. If Paolo didn't quite approve of the relationship, that was why. His cousin was an honorable man and knew that Vito was not behaving with complete honor. *If she's a victim, don't make her more of one.*

Vito was implying certain promises that he wouldn't keep, buying time with a woman who could be spending her affection more wisely elsewhere.

But Vito wanted her. His possessive desire was a kind of ferocious pulse beat inside him, territorial and unwavering. He was glad to get this settlement out of the way, glad to put another stage of the scandal behind them. Along with whatever arrangements he made for her when they eventually parted, she would have this very generous cushion for her future, but this was no more an end point to their liaison than the press conference had been.

She was his. He was keeping her. No one would stop him. If Paolo had tried, Vito might very well have shed his cousin's blood for the first time in twenty-odd years.

* * *

Gwyn only ever saw her stepbrother in casual clothes, usually wearing stubble and jeans. That's why it took her a full three pulse beats to realize the man who came in behind her lawyer, the man who was clean-shaven, wore a tailored suit as razor sharp as the Donatelli men's and said a grim, "About time," in a voice she knew was Travis.

"Oh, my God! What are you doing here?" She was taken aback, surprised by a light rush of excitement at seeing a familiar face. She almost stepped forward to hug him, but embarrassed realization hit at the same moment, along with the only reason she could imagine he would turn up so unexpectedly. "Is Henry okay?"

"He's fine. Worried sick about you," he said, sending a hostile glance around the conference room. "Why haven't you called him?"

"I…didn't know what to say. You told him I was okay, didn't you?"

"Are you? What is this?" He waved at the conference table where red folders had been set in front of a handful of chairs. "I told you not to sign anything without talking to me first."

"I texted you," she said.

"When I say talk, I mean talk, Gwyn."

Out of the corner of her eye, she saw Vito start forward with purpose, as if he took exception to Travis's patronizing attitude. Paolo stopped him with a hand on his chest and came forward with his own extended.

"Paolo Donatelli. And you are?"

"Travis Sanders. Gwyn's brother." He bit the words off.

Step, she almost clarified, but Travis was still talking.

"I'd like a word with her if you'll excuse us?" So dismissive to the men who owned the skyscraper.

Vito didn't move a muscle, stating implacably, "I'll stay."

Travis tried to stare Vito down. All the hairs on Gwyn's body stood up, electrified by the open animosity pinging back and forth between the men.

"Look, um—" She glanced to Paolo for help.

"Take as much time as you need," he said, flashing a look at his cousin, but only waving the lawyers from the room and pulling the door closed behind them.

Gwyn looked to Vito, but saw immediately there was no point in asking him to leave. The hostility radiating off him was palpable.

Licking her lips, she turned back to Travis. "I'm *sorry*," she said with deep sincerity. "It's true, I was avoiding you and Henry. This whole thing has been very humiliating. I feel horrible for what Henry and you must be going through."

Vito made a noise that she knew was an admonishment against apologizing for something that wasn't her fault.

"Is that why you haven't come home? Because you were embarrassed?"

She shrugged, as disconcerted by his forcefulness as by the implication that what she considered "home" was her home in his eyes, too.

"Is it?" Vito demanded from his position on the far end of the table. His hot glare was equally unnerving because he looked so stunned.

Hurt, even?

He must know she'd stayed for him. She swallowed, sending him a reassuring look before she turned back to her stepbrother.

"I stayed here for a lot of reasons, but I knew you must be furious—" she began.

"I'm furious because I'm worried, Gwyn!" he cut in. His dark face reddened with deep emotion and his hand waved in the air. "None of this is like you except the part where you refused to pick up the phone and ask me for help! Instead, you're relying on..."

His gaze tracked Vito as he came down the side of the table to where Gwyn stood, closing in behind her in a silent message that might have been a warning to Travis to mind his tone. There was such an air of menace as he looked at the man.

"What the hell is going on here?" Travis asked, shifting his disbelieving gaze to hers. "I mean, I know what it was supposed to look like. Anyone with half a brain can see you were backing Jensen into an admission that he set up the photos, but why are you still here now that that's accepted fact? Why didn't you come home after he was charged?"

"I—" She didn't know what to say. Somehow she was in Vito's grasp, her back against his front, one of his heavy hands on her hip, the other curled around her upper arm.

"Why do you care?" Vito remarked in a dangerous tone.

Travis lifted his gaze to a point past her shoulder, his eyes so cold and deadly, Gwyn tensed and held her breath.

"We're family," Travis said through lips that barely moved. "Maybe we're not related by blood, but we're family. Do you get me? She's not without connections. So whatever the hell you think you're doing with my sister, it ends now."

Family?

Gwyn was dumbfounded by Travis's reaction.

The whole moment was so supercharged with emotion, she almost couldn't speak, thoughts scattered. But these two pitbulls were about to take each other apart, so she covered Vito's hand on her arm and tried to ground out his aggression.

"It's okay," she told him, then turned to Travis. "Your worrying about me is really nice, but it's not necessary. I've been in good hands this whole time."

In her head that had seemed like a sensible thing to say, but the hands upon her tightened and Travis choked out, taking on a thunderstruck expression.

"Have you? Have you really?"

"Yes," she insisted, shifting enough so she could see Vito's stony expression over her shoulder. She wasn't sure what she had expected to see there, but not that cast of iron. For some reason it undermined her confidence in what she was saying. "Paolo and Vito have had my back this whole time."

"That's odd," Travis said, tone dripping sarcasm. "Because what it looks like to me is that a man in a position of power took advantage of a woman who was already in trouble, used her to keep his bank from taking a kick to its reputation, hung on to her to influence the settlement that was being negotiated—" he nodded at the folders on the table "—and *if* he keeps you here, will be using you for reasons that have become far more basic."

"Travis," she gasped, stabbed by his cruel assessment.

"I'm sorry, did I miss a wedding announcement?" Travis asked, flicking his gaze to Vito's. "Are your intentions honorable?"

Vito's hands fell away from her body and stripped her of her skin at the same time. *No.* She wouldn't let Travis ruin this. Why wasn't Vito explaining this wasn't cheap, physical gratification but something so much more?

Public humiliation was a cakewalk compared to losing the regard of people you cared about, she realized, as one man looked at her with pity and the other didn't meet her gaze at all.

"You've always thought I was a gold digger, Travis. Why are you upset to find me exactly where you expected me to be?" she threw out.

"Gwyn," Vito growled in protest while Travis's head snapped back.

"When did I ever call you that?"

"The wedding day. You said Mom and I—"

"I barely knew you!" No apology or denial, she noted. He just railed on. "Now I do and you're as green and idealistic as they come. He's taking advantage of you, Gwyn." And he looked genuinely outraged by it. If she wasn't so furious with him for ruining a good thing, she'd be touched.

"I'm an adult," she asserted. "Perfectly capable of deciding when and with whom I want a relationship."

"Oh, tell yourself that, but this isn't a 'relationship.' It's an arrangement. The most rudimentary kind. He's miles ahead of you and it's all calculated for his best interests, not yours. You will come away with some very pretty material items that I know will mean nothing to you because you are a woman looking for love, not lucre. You're better than this, Gwyn. Don't let him turn you into something you're not."

"You don't know anything about what we have," she said hotly, half turning to snag Vito with her glance, urging him—*insisting*—he defend himself. *Them.*

His jaw pulsed and he stared at Travis, not with heat, not with guilt. Blank.

It hurt. His silence gutted her and his refusal to appear insulted and furious shook her to the core.

"If you have any decency at all, you'll send her home with me," Travis said flatly. "She's better than this."

No, I'm not, Gwyn wanted to say. Maybe she even said it aloud. She knew she argued, "That's a stupid ultimatum. He doesn't have to prove anything to you. *I* decide whether I stay with him or not," she declared.

"Sign the papers when you're satisfied, not before," Vito said, more to Travis than to her, reaching to square one of the folders against the edge of the table, then sending a second look, this one blistering, back to Travis again. "You're wrong about my interfering in this. It's all been negotiated at arm's length, but I'll leave so I'm not a distraction while you finalize it."

"Vito!" Panic edged into her voice as she watched him circle toward the interior door. This wasn't really happening was it? "You're— This isn't—" *Over.* Was it? She couldn't finish the question, afraid she already knew the answer.

He paused, but he didn't turn around. "This was always going to happen, *cara*," he said gently. "You knew that."

She thought of the day when she'd been prepared to leave and had likened it to tearing off a bandage. But genuinely facing The End was a kind of pain she couldn't describe, like her soul was wrenched from her body. Her heart beat outside her chest.

She did the only thing she could. She turned on

Travis, the man who had marched in here talking like he cared about her and was destroying her life.

"Why would you do this to me? Do you resent me so much for taking some of your father's precious attention—"

"Gwyn," Vito said sharply, hand gripping the edge of the table with white knuckles, face grim. "*This was always going to happen.* Go home with your brother. Let him take care of you. I want to know you're safe there, not being harassed by the press or anyone else."

"Oh, do you?" she jeered. "What am I now? Not just a pawn, but a marble that gets picked up and taken home? *I* decide what happens to me!"

"Do whatever you want," he commanded. "But you're not coming home with me."

He might as well be throwing rocks at the dog that threatened to follow him. His words landed like sharp stones in her throat and her eyes and her glass heart, chipping and cracking it, leaving it in jagged broken pieces as he disappeared through the door and closed it with finality against her.

"Gwyn, I'm sorry," Travis said, touching her elbow.

She shook him off, distantly supposing she looked like someone had died in front of her because that's how she felt.

She had been miserable, absolutely devastated, when her nude photos had appeared. Vito had questioned her like a criminal and she had thought her life couldn't get any worse. Then he'd made everything better. He'd charmed and soothed and ignited her. He had made her fall in love with him. She had trusted him in ways she'd never let herself trust anyone, especially a man. She had offered her heart on a platter, let herself believe he cared for her at least a little…

But she meant nothing to him.

She hated him with everything in her. He was a bastard and she *hated* him.

At least, that's what she told herself.

The door he'd used to exit the conference room led into Paolo's office. His cousin stood up from his desk. "They're ready for us?"

"All I could see was your father," Vito told him numbly, trying to laugh it off, but ghosts were skimming across his skin, leaving it covered in gooseflesh. His chuckle came off his heart like a dry leaf. A kind of pain, the kind he would never let anyone, for any reason, inflict upon him, coursed like poison through his veins. "I can't be like mine, stealing something I'll end up destroying."

Incomprehension crystalized into understanding in Paolo's expression, maybe even something that might have been a protest, but Vito was already on the move again. If he didn't get out of here, he wouldn't be able to leave her.

"Finish without me. Give her whatever she wants."

CHAPTER TEN

NOT LONG AFTER her mother had married Henry, he had said to Gwyn, "Travis can teach you to drive."

Already far behind her age group in getting her license, Gwyn had declined, not wanting to look stupid in front of him, choosing instead to spend her hard-earned tip money on a couple of private lessons. She couldn't count the number of times Travis had offered to buy dinner over the years, but she'd always insisted on cooking. When she tried, she could think of four distinct times when he had asked whether she was looking for work because he'd heard about a particular position and was willing to recommend her. She'd always taken it as a criticism of the work she was doing or a favor that would make her indebted to him.

Not once had it ever occurred to her that he might give one solid damn about her.

He did. He might have blown up her relationship—*arrangement*—with Vito, but he was sorry. He was treating her like she was made of butterfly wings and soap bubbles, barely touching her, moving her with the gentle cadence of his voice. He told her that he shouldn't have waited for her to ask for help, but that he knew how important her independence was to her. He had wanted to respect her choices, but he couldn't watch her get hurt. He told her she could do better.

"I thought he cared about me," she finally broke her silence to say, as they flew first class back to Charleston.

"I know," he said after a surprised pause. She hadn't spoken since Vito had left the conference room, afraid her voice would crack and the rest of her control would follow. "And there are times when an affair like that is harmless. But you weren't coming into it as his equal. By that I mean the position you were in at the time, life experience, money, influence," he said with a glance from the corner of his eye. "You're a helluva better person."

"You don't know him," she mumbled into the drink he'd ordered her.

"I know him," Travis snorted. "It's like looking in a mirror."

For some reason that made her laugh, jaggedly and with fraught emotion, but as powerful and intimidating as she'd always found Travis, Vito was so much more. Everything she felt about him was massive and angsty and not the least bit brotherly.

Travis twisted his mouth and said, "Why is that funny? Shut up."

Which made her laugh more. Because the alternative was to cry and she'd wait to do that when she was alone.

He took her to Henry's and she really only meant to stay a week or so while she sorted out her life and got a job, but Henry practically begged her to stay. Then Travis walked her into an office a few blocks away and told her she was the comptroller for his friend's chain of high-end restaurants.

"Nepotism?" Her ego really needed to earn something on her own merit.

"Don't be like that. You're *over*qualified. But it's close, the money is good and no one will bother you. It's an excellent stepping stone," Travis urged. "It reestablishes you in the field which is something you need. He really needs someone who can upgrade his system and train the team to use it. You'll be doing him a favor."

"Right," she mumbled, but took the job.

It was awkward at first. Not so much at work. Everyone there was quite nice to her, but as she began moving around in public some people had the audacity to stare. Sometimes they asked outright if she was *that* woman. Usually if she replied, "Yes. Why?" it shut the interest down to a startled, "Just wondering."

Then there was the one day when she was feeling really thin-skinned and went off with the kind of fury that Vito had always warned her against.

It happened to be her mother's birthday. Her period had arrived that morning, severing any crazy illusions she had been nursing that she'd have a life-long tie with Vito. Then a knock at the door had announced her things from Italy. Not just the boxes from her flat that had gone into storage. *All* her things. Gowns that had hung next to Vito's suits. Scarves and scent and sandals.

Her gaze had scanned the entire inventory list, from eyebrow tweezers to toe rings, seeing novels and anklets and flower vases, but no mention of "Vito's heart."

She had asked the men to stack the boxes in the den, closed the door on them, made a huge breakfast for Henry, ate none of it herself and had cried in the shower before forcing herself to leave for work, already thirty minutes late.

So when she parked her car outside her new job and saw the cameras running at her like laser-shooting weapons in a sci-fi movie, she was already on her last nerve. A million babbled questions washed over her, all of them prompted by some shred of news in the Jensen case that she no longer cared anything about. But when one of the voices said, "We deserve to know everything that happened between you and Vittorio Donatelli," she lost it.

"You *deserve* to know? I'm supposed to betray his confidence and my own right to privacy and tell strangers about our personal relationship? What is wrong with you people? Do you understand what a relationship is? You rely on the other person *not* to talk about you. That's why humans make connections, so we have a safe place to be ourselves. Vito

Donatelli gave me that. That's what happened between us, okay? *Trust.* What a kinky, filthy concept, right? I'm sure it is to you!"

She used her elbows to get through the crowd, rather pleased when she heard grunts of startled pain and anxiety for their precious equipment.

"You don't deserve one damned thing."

Vito started to replay the moment where Gwyn gave the paparazzi a piece of her mind, but heard a squawk through the closed doors to Paolo's office.

He rose, not getting any work done anyway, and went through to find Lauren pacing in a light, bouncing step, patting the back of her fussing son.

"Hi," she said with a warm smile, coming across to kiss his cheeks. "Paolo's meeting me here with the other two, but I'm early. Sorry if we disturbed you. This one's fighting sleep even though he's overtired and grumpy." She wrinkled her nose at her son, then kissed his crinkled little chin.

Vito took him and settled him into what he privately labeled The Sleeper Hold. He'd learned it from watching his many relatives comfort his many infant relations. If a baby didn't take to the shoulder or a cradle hold in the arm, they wanted to lie on their stomach across a forearm, head pillowed in the crook of his elbow, limbs dangling.

Arturo made a stalwart effort to keep up his complaints, but settled in short order with one discontented kick of his leg and a weary sigh. Vito kept rubbing his back, pacing laconically to the window and back. Moments later, he held a warm, limp, sleeping baby.

"You're such a natural," Lauren said, stroking her son's hair, stopping short of the words he'd heard from countless women in his family. *Don't you want children of your own?*

"Paolo was visiting the old bank today," Vito said. "He took Roberto and Bianca?"

Lauren nodded. "Your aunt was meeting them there with a photographer."

Erecting this modern building and moving the Donatelli fortune into it had been a massive decision into which the entire family had weighed. While no one could dispute the practicality of bigger rooms and proper air-conditioning, or the SMART Boards and Wi-Fi and improved security, there was something to be said of the old financial district. The community was a tight one there. It had relied for centuries on old-fashioned networking in the narrow, cobbled streets of the city center.

It was how a young, beautiful daughter of an Italian banker had wound up catching the notice of a mafioso's son looking to launder his own father's ill-gotten gains.

"I've read there are hidden passageways under those old banks where secret deals were arranged back in the day. Paolo won't tell me if it's true."

"If he did, we would have to kill you," Vito said

casually. It was a myth that all of Milan enjoyed perpetuating.

"You bankers," she said, with a teasing grin. "You pretend to be so boring, but you're walking secrets, aren't you?"

Vito glanced down at the sleeping baby to disguise his reaction. "Hardly. What you see is what you get, *cara*."

"So you won't tell me yours," Lauren said after a brief, decidedly significant pause.

"Secrets? I have none to tell," he said, lifting his head and looking her in the eye as he spoke his bold-faced lie.

She tilted her head, but her gaze was soft with affection. "I've always imagined you fell in love with someone you couldn't have. That's why you won't marry and have children when you would make such a wonderful husband and father—"

"Lauren," he said gently. "I adore you. Let's keep it that way. Stop now."

"But then I saw you with Gwyn." Here was the woman who was strong enough to be Paolo's match. She rarely had to show this sort of steel because her sweet nature inevitably paved smooth streets wherever she went. But Paolo was not as domesticated as he appeared. A weak woman would not have fared well as his wife.

"Take him," he said, rolling Arturo into her arms. "We're not having this conversation." He started back to his office.

"I spent five years married to a man who didn't love me because I was afraid of what I felt for Paolo. Five years sleeping with the wrong man," she said to his back. "She'll find someone else you know."

He was at the door, feeling the latch like a knife hilt against this palm. A pain in his chest was the blade. He twisted it himself.

"She'll try to make babies with him," her voice continued in brutal purity behind him. "I did. Because she'll think that any man's baby is better than no baby at all…"

He almost had the door shut on her. Rude, but necessary.

Her voice elevated. "If you won't tell me, at least tell *her* why you're breaking her heart."

He pulled the door closed and turned the lock for good measure. Then he leaned his forehead upon it, blood moving like powdered glass in his arteries, the baby's body heat still imprinted on his aching arm.

CHAPTER ELEVEN

GWYN THOUGHT SHE was doing pretty well. It had been two months and most of the paparazzi vultures had learned that she lived a very boring life, going from Henry's to work to the grocery store to the dentist to the quickie oil change place. Even she was bored with her life.

Which is why she went on a date with a friend of her brother's. She told herself it was any number of things: getting back on the horse, research about a possible move to New York, interest in a career change to landscape architecture—hilarious. As if she had any interest in watching grass grow. But it was also an opportunity to eat in a restaurant where she didn't work, to see a jazz trio and wear one of the dresses she couldn't bring herself to discard.

She also told herself it was a test, to see if she could let any man other than Vito kiss her.

She was honest with him, told him up front that it was her first date since "it" had happened. He was good-natured, kept things casual and friendly, was a gentleman and a pleasant companion, making her laugh. He made her forget for moments at a time that she was pining and lost without the man she really loved.

But at the end of the night, when he moved to kiss her, she balked. It was instinctive. He wasn't Vito. It felt wrong.

He drew back, solemn and knowing, ruefully disappointed. "Not ready, huh?"

"I'm sorry."

"Don't be." He picked up her hand and kissed her bent knuckles. "I'll be back at the end of the year. We can go out again then. See if you feel differently."

"Thank you," she said, privately sighing. *But I won't.*

Then Henry turned on the porch light and they both chuckled.

Travis was at the breakfast table when she walked into the kitchen the next morning.

"Do not look at *anything*," he warned.

She knew the paparazzi had gone crazy. Cameras had been flashing around them all evening.

"He said we could go out again the next time he's in town." She poured a cup from the coffee he'd made. "But he doesn't realize how notorious I really am, does he?"

Travis said it wouldn't matter to his friend and as Gwyn went about her week, she wondered if anything mattered. It certainly hadn't mattered to Vito that she was dating other men.

Because deep in a sick corner of her soul, that was the real reason she had done it. She had hoped he would see one of those images that had been taken of her dining and dancing. She had hoped it would make him react.

Nothing.

Crickets.

Which was as painful and disheartening as the fact that she'd felt nothing for a perfectly nice man when he'd acted like he liked her, not just her face or body or the bare skin he'd seen online, but her.

With a shaky sigh, she looked down at the payments she was approving and wondered how many times she'd written her initials without taking in what she was actually signing. She started again.

When she walked outside, summer was announcing its intentions with a heat just this side of uncomfortable and a memo that humidity intended to climb to unbearable.

She dug her keys from her purse, ignoring the sound of a car door opening because it was likely yet another paparazzo—

"Cara."

Cupid's arrow, right through the heart. Sweetly painful, painfully sweet.

She turned to regard him and wished she'd taken a moment to find a bored expression. Instead, she was sure he read all the mixed feelings of welcome and yearning and hurt and betrayal. Why would he show up now, as she was finding ways to live without him?

Why like that? So iconic in one of his banker suits, cut to precision on his leanly sculpted form. He wore a hint of late-day stubble on his cheeks and his eyes were the color of morning light on mountain glaciers.

He stepped to the side and indicated the interior of his limo.

She sputtered, arms folding, aware of footsteps running toward them as some lurking paparazzo realized who she was talking to.

"Have dinner with me," Vito said, paying no attention to the click and whiz of the camera.

"It's four-thirty. I have my own car." She showed him her keys.

He turned and leaned down to speak to his driver, then slammed the door, walking toward her to hold out his palm.

"Really," she said, letting the full scope of her disbelief infuse the word. "Just take up where we left off? No."

"I want to talk to you."

"Does it occur to you that I might not want to talk to you?"

"That is a bluff." He met her gaze and there was a myriad of emotions behind that brutally beautiful face and somber expression. Knowledge shone in his eyes, knowledge of her and what he did to her, his patented arrogance, a kind of desolation that stopped her heart. Heat that made it jump and race again.

He took her keys from her limp fingers.

"I said I wanted to talk. You only need to listen."

He touched her elbow, turning her toward the parked cars. At the same time, he clicked the button so the lights on her hatchback flashed. Then he held the passenger door for her.

She hadn't sat on this side of her new car, which wasn't bottom of the line, but wasn't the kind of luxury Vito was used to. While he drove, she took out her phone long enough to punch in Henry's number, leaving a message that she wouldn't be home right away because she was going to dinner with Vittorio.

He glanced across as she dropped her phone into her purse.

"Things are well with your family? You're living with your stepfather. Is that because of the attention?"

He knew she hadn't moved into her own place? She hardly stalked him at all.

She shrugged. "He wants me there. I guess if there's a silver lining to the photos it's learning that I really do have a family. I know now exactly what other women mean when they say that older brothers are annoying. Your sisters must say that a lot."

His brow cocked at her cheeky remark, but he only said, "His protectiveness surprised me after the way you sounded so dismissive of him."

"Join the club," she snorted under her breath.

"He knows you went out with a man the other night?"

"I assume the whole world knows it, if you've heard about it." She reminded herself that it didn't matter that he was bringing it up—even if his voice had lowered to a tone that pretended to be casual, but was actually quite lethal. "He's a friend of Trav's so yes, he knows. He set it up." *Chew on that.*

"You had a nice time?" Again with the light tone, but his knuckles were white on the steering wheel.

"I don't talk about the men I date," she said flatly.

Silence for a full minute, until he stopped behind a line of traffic waiting for a light.

"No. You don't. I appreciate that, *cara*," he said softly, and this time his voice was filled with gravity and sincerity. "I know you've had offers for tell-alls. They must have been generous. You wouldn't have to work again, I'm sure."

She only turned her face to her side window. If he thought she was the least bit tempted in profiting from what they had shared, he really didn't know her at all.

"How do you like your job?" he asked.

"It's a job, Vito. It's no pin-up gig as Kevin Jensen's piece on the side. It's no mistress to a playboy banker. But it pays the bills."

"You're angry that I sent you away."

"I'm angry that you're here," she said, swinging her head around to glare at him. "My life was starting to look normal. Why stir it up again?"

Why? It was a fair question. One Vito couldn't answer. At least, not without admitting to himself that he was a very weak man.

"I want to explain why I sent you away," he said. Even though he had walked out on Lauren that day, telling himself she was wrong. Better to break ties cleanly, to let Gwyn move on with her life without knowing what kind of a near miss she'd had.

Why had he decided, after seeing her with another man, that he should let her know why she couldn't be with him? It was flawed logic.

He had wanted to see her again was the real answer. He could say that he wanted to talk and her to listen, but that was a lie. He wanted her to talk. He wanted her to relay every detail of the minutes she'd been away from him, the way she might have given him the highlights of her day visiting a museum, or conveyed a funny conversation she'd overheard on the street or simply traded views with him that might be more liberal than his own, but were always well thought out and left him with a broader view of the other side.

"I thought we were going to dinner," she said as he turned into the underground parking lot of the Donatelli International building.

"You said it was too early," he reminded, pulling into the spot reserved with his name, right next to the elevator. She scowled so mistrustfully at him, he had to chuckle. "I'm not going to kill you and eat you, *cara*."

No promises against licking and nibbling, of course.

It was all he could do not to pounce on her after he punched in the override code to get him to the floor he wanted. She had come out of her workplace with her jacket slung over her arm. Her black skirt was of a modest length, but narrow and stretchy, clinging to her hips and thighs. She wore a light green top that was so plain it was unremarkable, but the narrow belt at her waist gave it some traction across her bustline, emphasizing her hourglass figure. And those shoes with straps as narrow as her belt were positively erotic.

He hoped like hell he had paid for them, unsure why it mattered, just wanting to know she was still allowing him some place in her life.

She flicked her hair behind her shoulder, affecting cool composure, but her mouth was pulling at the corners as she said, "I know why you sent me away. It was an affair, nothing more. Like you said, it was always going to happen."

"Sì," he agreed, and the word moved up from his chest like gravel. "But for different reasons than you think."

The elevator opened into the private residential floor, where he and Paolo had suites and guest accommodations were made available to other family members. There was a private gym and indoor pool here, a dining lounge with views to the ocean that was closed because he was the only one here. Paolo's suite, where he had taken Lauren the night he'd told her that her husband was dead, was on the far side of the oversize foyer. Vito's was here, to his left, but before opening his door, he paused in the foyer and indicated the portrait on the wall.

It was a print of the original that had first hung in the old bank in Milan and now occupied the main lobby of the new tower.

"My great-grandfather," he said, looking at the man who'd been painted in his middle-aged prime wearing a brown plaid suit and a bowler hat.

He felt Gwyn's gaze touch him, questioning why this might be important, but she gave the portrait a proper study.

"He had two sons and five daughters, but only his sons inherited." He nodded at the two brothers who had cemented the foundation for what Banco Donatelli would become. "This one is my grandfather. His brother only had daughters. We've become more progressive and all share in the dividends now, but my uncle, Paolo's father, was recognized as his successor."

He moved to the photo of his grandfather with his wife and five children. It was a formal color photograph with the family posed for posterity, the fashions laughably dated. His grandfather had long sideburns and his pointed collar jutted out like wings against his tan suit and gold tie. His grandmother wore a floral print dress and Paolo's father, nearing twenty, was dressed like a newsboy. The four teenage girls wore identical dresses in a truly horrid purple.

"You Donatelli men get stamped out with the same mold generation after generation, don't you?"

She glanced from his great-grandfather, to his grandfather, then to his uncle and then to him. "The girls take after your grandmother. Except this one." She pointed at Antoinietta, barely twelve.

"Sì," he agreed, giving himself one last moment for reservations, but he had none. "That's why I look so much like a Donatelli. She is my actual mother."

Gwyn didn't know what to say, and Vito's profile gave nothing away as he moved to unlock a door and hold it for her.

She entered a private suite that was much smaller than his penthouse in Milan, but had such a similar decor, was stamped so indelibly as *his*, she felt as though she had come home.

"I don't understand," she told him, and the phrase covered many topics. Why had he told her that; why did it matter?

He moved to a photo on the wall in his lounge. The midnineties fashions weren't quite as painful as the seventies had been. A stout man wore a dark suit with a narrow tie that made his barrel chest seem more pronounced. His wife wore a black dress with a scoop neck. Young Vito actually pulled off the red suspenders over his white shirt, but his sisters' hairstyles, all wisped to look like a sitcom star's, were priceless.

She studied his image, realizing he looked… unlike the others.

Maybe she wouldn't have noticed it if he hadn't

told her this was not his biological family, but he was taller, leaner, more intense as he gazed into the camera while the rest of them beamed warmly. They seemed relaxed the way a family should when they were together, but he had that smoldering personality that never stopped emanating danger.

"*Mia famiglia.* I love them. My parents taught me generosity and acceptance. They love me every bit as much as they love their daughters. I would die for any of them. But my sisters have never been told," he said, making her swing her attention to him in surprise. "Paolo knows, but he's likely the only one in our generation or lower who does. He hasn't even told Lauren. I know some of my great-aunts and uncles have suspicions, but none has ever breathed a word..." He shook his head and shrugged. "This is something that was put in the vault and meant to be left there."

"Because your mother was young? Unmarried?" she guessed. His grandfather might have progressed to including his daughters in his will, but illegitimate babies had still been a scandal for a man in such a lofty position. It wasn't a big deal *now*, though. Was it? Why continue to hide it?

"My mother was eighteen. I'm a bastard, yes. And I won't tell you the name of my father, but that's for your own protection as much as mine. He was mafioso, *cara*. A truly dangerous and reprehensible man."

She blinked, shocked, and moved blindly to sit on the edge of the sofa. "How—?"

"—does the daughter of a banker get mixed up with a thug? He singled her out. I'm sure he had his moments of charm. I've seen photos and I imagine any woman would call him attractive. According to my uncle, my mother might as well have been the youngest daughter of a church minister, rebelling at her father's attempts to keep her cloistered. My grandfather was ready to disown her, but my uncle kept fighting to bring her home. I mean that literally. He had scars. She went back, regardless. Again and again."

"Got pregnant."

"Indeed." He pushed his hands into his pockets, rocked on his heels, scowl remote and dark. "Even though she came away bruised at different times. I will never understand—"

His profile was hard and sharp.

"She was late into her pregnancy when he bashed her around and she left for the last time. She called my uncle to come take her to the hospital, but she was far into labor when he got there. He caught me and held her as she died. She begged him to keep me from my father. If you could have seen his face when he told me these things…"

"Oh, Vito," she breathed, rising to go to him, hand reaching for his arm, but he was a statue, unmoved by her touch, barely seeming to breathe, face still and harsh as though carved into marble.

"This is what I am, *cara.* A mixture of impetuous Donatelli rebellion—have you met Paolo? I have that same cursed need to dominate and it is a monumental task to hold all of that back. Then I have this streak of brutality on top of it. My father killed people. And the dead ones are the victims who got off easy. His other son turned out as conscienceless, trafficking in women and drugs, winding up dead in the gutter outside his own home, like a rat. I even have a nephew. He's already been arrested for assault. There but for the grace of the Donatelli family go I."

"Vito," she chided. He didn't really think he would have turned out like that, did he? She frowned, hurting for him, feeling how tortured his soul was by a bloodline he didn't want and couldn't escape.

He ran his hand down his face. "I cannot perpetuate that sickness into another generation, not into the very family that took me in, kept me this side of the law and out of the hands of a man who would have turned me into himself. I *won't* risk it. Do you understand? Do you see now why I can't marry you and give you that dream I see in your eyes every time you rock a baby or hold a child's hand?"

She lowered her eyes, aching inside. He saw through her every single time.

"When your brother came to Milan that day," he said heavily, "all I could think was that it was better to let our separation happen then, before you were pregnant with an abomination—"

"Don't say that!"

He held up a hand. "But it tortures me, *cara*, that he made it sound like you were only a convenience to me. Our affair served many purposes, not all of them romantic, *sì*. That's true. But to let you think that was all it was is a lie. We are honest with one another if nothing else, are we not?"

"Are we?" she asked, mind reeling from all he'd told her, which made certain suspicions rise that were so sweet and fragile she barely let herself touch them. But why would he tell her all this, with that tortured look on his face, if he didn't care for her, trust her, not just a little, but a lot.

"Does some part of this sound made-up to you?" he asked, voice chilling and shoulders going back.

She made a noise. "Well, it is quite a story. But I do believe you. No, I'm questioning why you've told me."

She thought back to that day in the elevator when he'd been so angry at what she hadn't been able to see in him. All this time he'd presented her with the thick wall of the vault that fronted the man inside. Of course she'd had trouble seeing his true thoughts and feelings.

But now, now she thought she saw very clearly. It wasn't just wishful thinking, was it?

"I just explained," he said testily. "I didn't want you hurting unnecessarily."

"So I'm supposed to not hurt when you leave again? Secure in the knowledge that your rejection is for my own good? You know I love you, don't you?" There. She flung her own vault wide open, crashing it into the wall.

He flinched, dragging in air like he'd taken a knife to the lung. "I hoped that you didn't," he said through his teeth.

"Oh! Another lie!" she charged, stabbing a finger at his chest, hard enough to hurt her fingernail.

He grabbed her hand and glared, dark brows a fierce line. "I'm not lying!"

"You knew I was in love with you and you sent me away to get over it, but the minute you thought I might, you came back to see exactly how deep my feelings went. This—" she pulled free of his grip and pointed wildly to encompass all the photos he'd shown her "—is a test."

"Untrue. I'm explaining to you why I can't marry you and give you the family you've always wanted."

"Fine. I accept," she said, crossing her arms.

He grew cautious. "Accept what?"

"That we'll never marry and have children. Maybe we can talk about adopting someday, but that's not a condition. I'll accept simply living together without all those picket-fence trappings I always wanted."

"No!" he growled. "That's not what I'm saying. You deserve those things, Gwyn. Your brother is right. That's why—" He cut himself off with an impatient noise, palm scraping up his cheek, creating a raspy sound.

"So I should go marry another man and have his babies?" she confirmed.

"No! Damn you, no. I hated seeing you with that

man. It made me sick. No. And damn you for forcing me to admit that." He stalked away a few steps, hand raking into his hair. "I'm trying to think of you, Gwyn, but I keep acting for myself. That is who I am. Greedy. Selfish." He pivoted. "Don't you see that's what I'm trying to protect you from? I want that deal you're offering. I want to take you into my home as my lover and shortchange you on all the things you have a right to. What does that make me? How could you love someone like that?"

"What kind of man are you really?" she cried. "One who blames himself for his mother's death?"

He jerked a little in surprise, said, "No," but without conviction. Then hitched a shoulder. "Perhaps. A little. Everyone, the aunts and uncles who knew, always looked at me as if… I used to fight with Paolo. A lot. But then my uncle told me about this and I knew I had to contain this part of myself. Stamp it out as much as possible."

"And you have," she told him. "Are you likely to hit me, Vito?"

"No," he said, his contempt for men who would do such a thing thick in the word.

"What if I provoke you? What if I push you?" she asked, coming across to give him a light shove in the middle of his chest.

He caught her hands and easily twisted her arms behind her back, hauling her close in such a swift move they both released a little, "Ha," as their bodies lightly slammed together.

She tested his hold. “Now what are you going to do to me?” she said, but softly. Knowingly. She was never frightened here, only eager with anticipation.

“Kiss you,” he answered. “Make love to you.”

“Love me?” she suggested. Begged.

He lowered his head with a groan, capturing her mouth in a way that instantly owned, but gave at the same time. Anointed. Worshipped. His kiss was almost chaste in its sweetness, but so carnal they couldn’t help running their tongues together and opening to deepen the kiss until they were both breathless.

Then he released her arms and tucked her head against his chest where his heart slammed, his strong arms enfolding her to him.

She stroked his sides, soothing the beast.

“I could never hurt you, Gwyn. I wanted to carve out my own heart when I saw the way you looked at me that day you left Milan. The thought that I’d left you feeling anything but confident in how very lovable you are was intolerable. I do love you.” He touched his lips to her ear. “I love you in ways I didn’t know it was possible to love, with my body, with my breath. I ache with love for you every night and every day.”

She closed her eyes, savoring the sting of joyous tears. Threading her arms around him, she held on to him and the moment. The strength that had sustained her and protected her and would be hers. Because she would fight for this.

Him.

"Vito, how did the Donatellis keep you this side of the law?"

"I don't know," he muttered, digging his fingers into her hair, petting her like he was comforting himself. "A million ways, I suppose. Redirection, distraction, love."

"I love you," she drew back to say.

His hold on her flexed and he swallowed. "She loved him. He didn't change."

"Look what she was starting with," she said wryly. "What makes you think a child of yours couldn't be molded the way you were? Especially if he or she started out loved, the way you did?"

"Cara—" It was both protest and longing.

"It's not a deal breaker, I swear. I'm just saying you shouldn't write off your genes as all bad. Either way, I'm yours. You're stuck with me, understand?"

"Your brother is never going to— Screw it," he muttered, ducking abruptly to scoop her legs out from under her and give her a toss, catching her in the cradle of his arms, high against his chest. "We're getting married. Maybe we will adopt, but I'm not having you walk around without my ring. No one will call you anything but my wife."

"Was that a proposal? Because I missed the part where I was asked," she said, but it was hard to sound tart when she was grinning and his neck smelled good and she wanted to crawl inside his clothes.

Under his skin. "I missed you," she said against his Adam's apple, voice thready with need.

"I'm half a man without you," he said as he strode into the bedroom and placed her on his bed. "I'm only the worst parts of myself. Angry, jealous, miserable." He yanked his shirt open as he pulled it from his pants. "You understand what kind of possessive bastard you're consigning yourself to, don't you?"

"I'd like to say it's my choice, but I don't think I've ever had one." She lifted her hips to reach her zipper, then working her skirt down, enjoying the way his chest swelled at the sight of her bared legs. He hurried to finish undressing. "It has to be you or no one," she told him.

"Are you still on the pill?" he asked.

She nodded while she released the belt that she'd worn over her shirt, but she caught the little something that passed over his expression. It was a brief hesitation, words that rose but were second-guessed. One day, she knew from that tiny moment of betrayed thought, one day he would be ready to think about children. It was okay that today wasn't that day. She wanted him to herself for a little while, anyway.

He skimmed her undies away and settled his hot body over her, his hips between her legs. One arm reached to help her finish pushing off her top. "This is pretty," he said of her bra, tracing the edge of the blue-green lace. "It can stay for now."

He leaned to kiss her, but she drew back, needing to know.

"Does it bother you that so many men have seen me naked?"

"That will always bother me, *cara*. Not just because I am a jealous Neanderthal of a man, but because it hurt you so very badly. I would do *anything* to make that go away for you."

She traced her fingertips along his temple, down the side of his face, then cupped the side of his neck. "But we might not have found each other if that hadn't happened. And you wouldn't be here at all if your mother and father hadn't happened. Life is never going to be perfect and tidy, you know. Bad things can happen. We can only do our best with what we're given."

"Are you giving yourself to me?"

"I am," she said solemnly.

Excitement lit his eyes, but his kiss was tender. "Then I will do my best with you. That is a promise, *mia bella*." He settled his hips low and his hard, glorious length slid into her, slid home, making her groan in welcome. This was where they both belonged.

"Ti amo tanto," he groaned. *I love you so much.*

And later, when they were debating whether to rise and go out to eat, both completely lacking the will to move any more than a hand to caress a collarbone or turn their lips into each other's skin, her ringtone sounded from the other room.

Leaning off the bed for his pants, Vito pulled out his own phone and dialed, saying a moment later, "She's not coming home tonight. We'll come by your father's in the morning on the way to the jewelry store. I'll ask for her hand like a proper suitor. Good enough?"

It must have been because he hung up after one grumbled word from a voice she recognized as Trav's.

"I told you he's annoying," she said.

Vito set aside his phone and gathered her beneath him, bracing himself on his elbow above her, just looking at her in the half light of dusk coming through the uncovered windows.

"I like it, *tesoro*. I'm a competitive man. I will enjoy treating you so well he is forced to eat his words again and again."

She burst out laughing, not asking where his edges and superiority complex came from. At least he was using his naturally dominant nature for good instead of evil.

"I do love you, you know," she told him, gazing into his eyes. "I love you because you told me. You trust me. That means so much."

"I never imagined telling anyone." He frowned across the room, into the middle distance. "It's not about protecting me anymore, but protecting the bank. This could be a very big problem for the family."

"I'll never tell a soul, I promise."

"I know." His brows gave a little pull, like she was stating the obvious. "I knew when I came here that even if you were repelled, the secret would always be safe with you."

She petted his cheek, smoothing his rough stubble, chiding, "But I will take every opportunity to point out things like the fact that you have a crazy fierce capacity for loyalty. If your son or daughter had the same, we'd have nothing to worry about."

His beautiful mouth pursed. "One of the first things I admired about you was that fighting spirit of yours."

"Really?" She tussled with him and he let her win, so she had him on his back and she sat straddled over his thighs. But rather than crow with triumph as she pinned his big hands to the mattress, she leaned down to say against his lazy, satisfied grin, "You changed my world and I'm going to change yours."

"Vows to live by, *mia bella*. I do."

EPILOGUE

"DON'T YOU DARE, you little streaker!" Gwyn said, but her daughter had figured out that her mother was handicapped by a belly the size of Nebraska. She slithered away and left Gwyn on her knees holding a towel and a clean diaper.

"Vito!" Gwyn cried, and awkwardly clambered to her feet, waddling after her just-turned-two-year-old into the hall.

Antoinietta made her way down the stairs with determined little feet, hands gripping each of the uprights in turn, always tenacious about getting what she wanted, but willing to play by the rules once they were given to her.

Vito made no effort to come up to the girl, just stood at the bottom with his hands on his hips. "You really take after your mother, don't you?"

"Oh, you're funny," Gwyn told him, narrowing her eyes in a promise of retribution. "I told her who was coming for dinner. It was supposed to be an inducement to get her into her clothes, but…" She waved to indicate how well that had worked.

"Bea!" Toni called, trying to dodge her father as he made a grab for her at the bottom of the stairs. Then she said a very stern, "No, Papa," when he caught her and carried her up the stairs. The higher he went, the more she struggled and the louder she said, *"Down."*

"Yeah, that's all me," Gwyn said as he took the diaper from her. Their daughter was making a very serious effort to get out of his hold, squirming so hard her face was red, pudgy fists white and tiny brows screwed up with stubborn resolve.

"She's *two*," Vito said.

"She's *yours*," Gwyn said, chuckling when that actually made him close his arms even more tenderly around his adamant little girl.

"She is," he said proudly, and proceeded to speak in a calm voice, explaining that her cousins would be here soon, but she had to dress first.

He wrangled her into her clothes amid a great deal of negotiating and, *"Me do!"*

The bell rang as Vito carried her down the stairs a few minutes later and Toni's excitement soared as Bianca and the boys entered. She spared a moment to hug and kiss the adults, but her adulation was reserved for her true hero, Roberto, her partner in mischief, Arturo, and her dearest and most beloved Bianca.

"Bea." She hugged the girl who knelt to hug her back with every warm and sweet bone in her body.

Gwyn was almost as excited as her daughter when

family came over. Henry now saw the advantage of a tablet and connected with them online when he wasn't actually staying at the apartment he'd bought nearby, so he could visit in person and watch his granddaughter grow up. He was flying in next week, anticipating the new baby would be with them. Even Travis had made a point of coming with his father for Christmas this year, since Gwyn had been too far along to travel.

Tonight it was Vito's turn for having family over. All of Vito's relations had made her feel welcome, Vito's parents especially, but Lauren was like a sister to Gwyn. Now that they were both pregnant, they were even closer than ever.

As for the man who was her boss again, after contracting her for a special project he'd offered to her a year ago? She didn't find him nearly as formidable.

"You're as much of a comedian as your cousin, aren't you?" she said to Paolo as he set a bag she recognized inside the door. It was the birthing kit he'd prepared when they had come to the house on Lake Como and Lauren had delivered Arturo. "I'm warning you right now, if your wife has her baby in my home, when I am already eleven months pregnant—" It was an exaggeration, but that was how she felt.

Paolo cut her off by kissing her cheek. "I brought it for Vito."

"Ha!"

"Bite your tongue," Vito muttered.

"The doctor said I'm at least two weeks away,"

Lauren assured them and they all groaned and rolled their eyes. “But honestly, Gwyn. The second one comes faster.”

“So I can count on thirty-six hours reducing to thirty?” Gwyn joked.

“Cara,” Vito protested. He had been appalled, genuinely upset that all the pleasure they gave each other had resulted in so much pain for her, but Toni was such a gift Gwyn was more than willing to go through it again to meet the next addition to their family. In fact, she had a feeling it would be sooner than later. One of the reasons she had invited them for dinner was because she had that low, dull ache in her pelvis that had sat with her for two days before her labor had started for real with Toni.

Soon, she knew, she’d be tied up with a newborn and not entertaining for a while, so she wanted a proper visit with this family she enjoyed so much while she had the time.

Sure enough, a few hours later, as she and Lauren were drying dishes, the first pain hit, a nice strong one that took her breath.

“Vito,” Lauren called as she took the plate from Gwyn’s hand. “We’re going to take Toni home with us. You and your wife have a date with a midwife.”

They made that date, with no time to spare. Second babies did come faster and Vito almost had to eat his smug words to Paolo as they’d left, about how some men got their wives to the hospital before their children delivered. His son arrived as Gwyn was being admitted, caught by a startled ER nurse who barely had time to pull the curtain.

"Do you mind?" Gwyn asked Vito when she was settled in the maternity ward, pronounced healthy along with their son, but staying for overnight observation. "That he's a boy, I mean?"

"Why would I mind?" he asked, lifting a sharp gaze from studying the boy.

"You wanted a girl with Toni. I thought…" She had taken it to mean he believed girls were less likely to develop undesirable behaviors.

"Because I wanted to name her Antoinietta. I knew my mother would be touched to have her sister remembered and she is."

"You're not worried your son will be like—"

"Me?" he cut in, mouth twisting into a wry smirk. "I'm counting on it."

She had to chuckle at that, and leaned forward to kiss him. "Me, too."

* * * * *

Turn the page for an exclusive extract of
SLEEPLESS IN MANHATTAN,
the first book in USA TODAY *bestselling author*
Sarah Morgan's enthralling new trilogy,
FROM MANHATTAN WITH LOVE*!*

PAIGE STOOD FOR a moment, thinking how unpredictable life was.

Who would have thought that herself, Eva and Frankie losing their jobs would have turned out so well?

Urban Genie existed only because life had laid a twist in her path.

Change had been forced on her, but it had proved to be a good thing.

Instead of fighting it, she should embrace it.

What had Jake said?

Sometimes you have to let life happen.

Maybe she should try to do that a bit more.

And maybe one day she'd look back and realize that *not* being with Jake was the best thing that could have happened—because if she'd been with Jake she wouldn't have met—

Who?

Would she ever meet someone who made her feel the way Jake did?

She stood leaning on the railing, gazing at the city she loved.

The lights of Manhattan sparkled like a thousand stars against a midnight sky and now, finally, as the last of the guests made their way to the elevators, she allowed herself a moment to enjoy it.

"Time to relax and celebrate, I think."

Jake's voice came from behind her and she turned to find him holding two glasses of champagne. He handed her one. "To Urban Genie."

"I don't drink while I'm working." And while Jake was present this was definitely still work.

She knew better than to lower her guard a second time.

"The guests have gone. You're no longer working. Your job is done."

"I'm not off duty until the clear-up has finished." And then tomorrow would be the follow-up, the post-mortem. Discussions on what they might have done differently. They'd unpick every part of the event and put it back together again. By the time they'd finished they'd have found every weak spot and strengthened it.

"I don't think one glass of champagne is going to impair your ability to supervise that. Congratulations." He tapped his glass against hers. "Spectacular. Any new business leads?"

"Plenty. First up is a baby shower next week. Not much time to prepare, but it's a good event."

He winced. "A baby shower is *good*?"

"Yes. Partly because the woman throwing it for her pregnant colleague is CEO of a fashion importer. But all business is good."

"Chase Adams is impressed. By tomorrow word will have got around that Urban Genie is the best event concierge company in Manhattan. Prepare to be busy."

"I'm prepared."

His praise warmed her. Her heart lifted.

He stood next to her and the brush of his sleeve against her bare arm made her shiver.

His gaze collided briefly with hers and she thought she saw a blaze of heat, but then he looked away and she did, too, her face burning.

She was doing it again. Imagining things.

And it had to stop.

It had to stop right now.

No more embarrassing herself. No more embarrassing *him*.

She turned her head to look at him but he was staring straight ahead, his handsome face blank of expression.

"Thank you," she said.

"For what?"

"For asking us to do this. For giving us free rein and no budget. For trusting us. For inviting influential people and decision-makers. For making Urban Genie happen." She realized how much she owed him. "I hate accepting help—"

"I know, but that isn't what happened here. You did it yourself, Paige."

"But I wouldn't have been able to do it without you. I'm grateful. If you hadn't suggested it, pushed me that night on the terrace, I wouldn't have done it." She breathed in. Now was as good a time as any to say everything that needed to be said. And if she said it aloud maybe it would help both of them. "There's something else—" She saw him tense and felt a flash of guilt that he felt the need to be defensive around her. *Definitely* time to clear the air. "I owe you an apology."

"For what?"

"For misreading the situation the other night. For making things awkward between us. I was…" She hesitated, trying to find the right words. "I guess you could say I was doing an Eva. I was looking for things that weren't there. I was close to panic and you were trying to distract me. I understand that now. I don't want you feeling that you have to avoid me, or be careful around me. I'd never want that. I—"

"Don't. Don't apologize."

He gripped the railing and she noticed his knuckles were white.

"I wanted to clear it up, that's all. It was a kiss. Didn't mean anything. Two people trapped in an elevator, one of whom was feeling vulnerable." *Shut up right now, Paige.* "I know I'm not your type. I know you don't have those feelings. I'm like your little sister. I get that. So—"

"Oh, for— *Seriously?*" He interrupted her with a low growl and finally turned to face her. "After what happened the other night you really think I see you as *a little sister*? You think I could kiss you that way if I felt like that about you?"

She stared at him, her heart drumming a rhythm against her chest. "I thought— You said— I thought you saw me that way."

"Yeah, well, I tried." He gave a humorless laugh and drained his champagne in one mouthful. "God knows, I tried. I've done everything short of asking Matt for a baby photo of you and sticking that to my wall. Nothing works. And do you know why? Because I *do* have feelings, you're *not* little and you're not my damn *sister*."

Shock struck her like a bolt of lightning.

They were the only two people left on the terrace. Just them and the Manhattan night. The buildings rose around them—dark shapes enveloping them in intimate shadows and the shimmer of light.

The storm clouds were gathering, creating ominous shadows in the dark sky.

The sudden lick of wind held the promise of rain.

Paige was oblivious. The sky might have come crashing down and she wouldn't have noticed.

Her mouth was so dry she could hardly form the words. "But if you feel that way, if you do have feelings, why do you keep saying—" She stumbled over the words, confused. "Why haven't you ever done anything about it?"

"Why do you think?"

There was a cynical, bitter edge to Jake's tone that didn't fit the nature of their conversation. None of the pieces fitted. She couldn't think. Everything about her had ceased to function.

"Because of Matt?"

"Partly. He'd kick my butt. And I wouldn't blame him." He stared down at his hands, as if they were something that didn't belong to him. As if he was worried about what they might do.

"Because you're not interested in relationships—or 'complications' as you call them?"

"Exactly."

"But sex doesn't have to be a relationship. It can just be sex. You said so yourself."

"Not with you."

His tone was harsh and she took a step back, shocked. They'd often argued, baited each other, but she'd never heard that edge of steel in his voice before.

"Why? What's different about me?"

"I'm not going to screw you and walk away, Paige. That's not going to happen."

"Because of our friendship? Because you're worried it would be awkward?"

"Yeah, that, too."

"Too? What else?" She stared at him, bemused.

He was silent.

"Jake? What else?"

He swore under his breath. "Because I care about

you. I don't want to hurt you. There's already been enough damage to your heart. You don't need more."

The first raindrops started to fall.

Paige was still oblivious.

Her head spun with questions. *Where? What? Why? How much?* "So you— Wait—" She struggled to make sense of it. "You're saying that you've been *protecting* me? No. That can't be true. You're the only one who *doesn't* protect me. When everyone else is wrapping me in cotton wool, you handle me as though you're throwing the first pitch at a game."

He didn't protect her. He *didn't*. Not Jake.

She waited for him to agree with her, to confirm that he didn't protect her.

He was silent.

There was a throbbing in her head. She lifted her fingers to her forehead and rubbed. The storm was closing in—she could feel it. And not just in the sky above her.

"I *know* you don't protect me." She tried to focus, tried to examine the information and shook her head. "Just the other night, when we found out we'd lost our jobs, Matt was sympathetic but you were brutal. I was ready to cry, but you made me so *angry* and—" She stared at him, understanding. She felt the color drain from her face. "You did it on purpose. You made me angry on purpose."

"You get more done when you're angry," he said flatly. "And you needed to get things done."

No denial.

He'd goaded her. Galvanized her into action.

"You challenge every idea I have." She felt dizzy. "We fight. All the time. If I say something is black, you say it's white."

He stood in silence, not bothering to deny it, and she shook her head in disbelief.

"You *make* me angry. You do that on purpose. Because if I'm angry with you, then I'm not—" She'd been blind. She breathed hard, adjusting to this new picture of their relationship. The first boom of thunder split the air but she ignored it. "How long? How long, Jake?"

"How long, what?" He yanked at his bow tie with impatient fingers.

His gaze shifted from hers. He looked like a man who wanted to be anywhere but with her.

"How long have you cared? How long have you been p-protecting me?" She stumbled over the word—and the thought.

He ran his hand over his jaw. "Since I walked through the door of that damn hospital room and saw you sitting on the bed in your Snoopy T-shirt, with that enormous smile on your face. You were so brave. The most frightened brave person I'd ever seen. And you tried so hard not to let anyone see it. I have *always* protected you, Paige. Except for the other night, when I let my guard down."

But he'd been protecting her then, too. He'd been taking care of her when she'd been so terrified she hadn't known what to do.

"So you thought I was brave, but not strong? Not strong enough to cope alone without protection? I don't understand. I thought you weren't interested, that you didn't want this, and now I discover—" It was a struggle to process it. "So this whole time you *did* care about me. You *do*."

Rain was falling steadily now, landing in droplets on his jacket and her hair.

"Paige—"

"The kiss the other night—"

"Was a mistake."

"But it was real. It wasn't because I was a pair of red lips in an elevator. All these days, months, *years* I've been telling myself you didn't feel anything. All the time I've been confused because my instincts were so wrong and I couldn't understand why. But now I do. They weren't wrong. *I* wasn't wrong."

"Maybe you weren't."

"So why let me think that?"

"Because it was easier."

"Easier than what? Telling me the truth? News flash—and, by the way, I thought you knew this—I don't want to be protected. I want to live my life. You're the one who's always telling me to take more risks."

"Yeah, well, that proves you shouldn't listen to anything I tell you. We should go inside before you catch pneumonia."

He eased away from the railings and she caught his arm.

"I'll go inside when I decide to go inside." The rain was soaking her skin. "What happens now?"

"Nothing. I know you don't want to be protected but that's tough, Paige, because that's what I'm doing. I'm not what you're looking for and I never have been. We don't want the same thing. There's a car waiting downstairs to take you and the other two home. Make sure you use it."

Without giving her a chance to respond, Jake strode away from her toward the bank of elevators and left her standing there, alone in the glittering cityscape, watching the entire shape of her life change. Another twist. Another turn. The unexpected.

Don't miss SLEEPLESS IN MANHATTAN
by Sarah Morgan,
available from HQN Books.

COMING NEXT MONTH FROM

HARLEQUIN *Presents*®

Available July 19, 2016

#3449 THE DI SIONE SECRET BABY

The Billionaire's Legacy

by Maya Blake

Charity CEO Allegra Di Sione can't fail in her mission to retrieve her grandfather's beloved Fabergé box from Sheikh Rahim Al-Hadi, which is why she gets caught in Rahim's sumptuous bedroom trying to steal it!

#3450 CARIDES'S FORGOTTEN WIFE

by Maisey Yates

After a car accident erases his memories, Leon Carides remembers nothing, except Rose's sparkling blue eyes. Now he'll do anything to claim the wife he'd left behind...including taking her to his bed!

#3451 THE PLAYBOY'S RUTHLESS PURSUIT

Rich, Ruthless and Renowned

by Miranda Lee

Playboy tycoon Jeremy Barker-Whittle isn't short on stunning women, but Alice Waterhouse is a challenge he can't refuse. But when he discovers Alice's carefully guarded innocence, he must forget this delicate beauty...until Alice shocks him by offering her virginity!

#3452 CROWNED FOR THE PRINCE'S HEIR

One Night With Consequences

by Sharon Kendrick

Dress designer Lisa Bailey broke off her fling with Luc, knowing her affair with the royal could never go anywhere. But after a one-off date "for old times' sake," there are consequences that tie her to Luc forever...

HPCNM0716RA

#3453 MARRYING HER ROYAL ENEMY

Kingdoms & Crowns

by Jennifer Hayward

Most women would kill to be draped in ivory and walking up the aisle toward King Kostas Laskos. But Stella Constantinides naively bared her heart to Kostas to disastrous effect once before and this feisty princess refuses to be his pawn ever again.

#3454 HIS MISTRESS FOR A WEEK

by Melanie Milburne

Years ago, Clementine Scott clashed spectacularly with arrogant architect Alistair Hawthorne and swore she'd never have anything to do with him again! But when Clem's brother disappears with Alistair's stepsister, she's forced to go with Alastair to Monte Carlo to retrieve them!

#3455 IN THE SHEIKH'S SERVICE

by Susan Stephens

Sheikh Shazim Al Q'Aqabi must resist his instant attraction to mysterious dancer Isla Sinclair, for duty is Shazim's only mistress. Until Isla is revealed as the prize winner who will travel to the desert to work with him...making their chemistry impossible to ignore.

#3456 CLAIMING HIS WEDDING NIGHT

by Louise Fuller

Addie Farrell's marriage to casino magnate Malachi King lasted exactly one day, until she discovered their love was a sham. Now Addie must prepare to face her husband—and their dangerously seductive chemistry—once again!

SPECIAL EXCERPT FROM

HARLEQUIN *Presents*®

A Harlequin Presents® brand-new eight-book series,
The Billionaire's Legacy: *the search for truth and the promise of passion continues…*

Charity CEO Allegra Di Sione can't fail in her mission to retrieve her grandfather's beloved box from Sheikh Rahim Al-Hadi—which is why she gets caught in Rahim's sumptuous bedroom trying to steal it!

Read on for a sneak preview of
THE DI SIONE SECRET BABY

"I came here to set a few things straight with you," Rahim sneered, deeply resentful that she'd led him to question himself when there was no doubt where his destiny lay. "You thought what happened in Dar-Aman wouldn't go unchallenged. You were wrong."

Allegra's hand jerked to her stomach, her eyes more vivid against her ashen colour. "No. Please…"

From across the room, Rahim saw her sway. With a curse, he charged forward and caught her as her legs gave way. It occurred to him then that she hadn't answered him when he'd asked what ailed her. Swinging her up into his arms, he carried her to the sofa and laid her down.

With a low moan, she tried to get up. Rahim stayed her with a firm hand. "I'm going to get you some water. Then you'll tell me what's wrong with you. And what the hell you're doing giving long speeches and photo ops when you should be in bed."

HPEXP0716R

Her mouth pursed mutinously for a moment before she gave a small nod.

Rising, he crossed to the bar and poured a glass of water. She'd sat up by the time he returned. Silently she took the water and sipped, her wary eyes following him as he sat on the sturdy coffee table directly in front of her.

"Now tell me what's wrong with you."

The sleek knot at her nape had come undone during the journey to the sofa, and twin falls of chocolate-brown hair framed her face as she bent her head. Rahim gritted his teeth against the urge to brush it back, soothe whatever was troubling her, reassure her that he meant her no harm.

He was so busy fighting his baser urges, and sternly reminding himself that he was in the right and she in the wrong, that he didn't hear her whispered words.

"What did you say?"

Her jerky inhale wobbled the glass in her hands. "I said I'm not sick, but I can't go to prison because I'm pregnant." She raised her head then and stared back at him with eyes black with despair. "I'm carrying your child, Rahim."

THE WORLD IS BETTER WITH *Romance*

Harlequin has everything from contemporary, passionate and heartwarming to suspenseful and inspirational stories.

Whatever your mood, we have a romance just for you!

Connect with us to find your next great read, special offers and more.

/HarlequinBooks

@HarlequinBooks

www.HarlequinBlog.com

www.Harlequin.com/Newsletters

SERIESHALOAD2015